PADDINGTON™
– the Story of the Movie

D0166865

PADDINGTON™
– the Story of the Movie

Jeanne Willis

HarperCollins *Children's Books*

First published in paperback in Great Britain by
HarperCollins *Children's Books* in 2014
HarperCollins *Children's Books* is a division of HarperCollins *Publishers* Ltd.
77-85 Fulham Palace Road, Hammersmith, London W6 8JB.

www.harpercollins.co.uk

1

Written by Jeanne Willis
Based on the Paddington novels written and created by Michael Bond
PADDINGTON™ and PADDINGTON BEAR™ © Paddington and Company
Limited / STUDIOCANAL S. A. 2014

ISBN 978-0-00-759275-3

Typeset in Bembo by Palimpsest Book Production Ltd, Falkirk, Stirlingshire
Printed and bound in England by Clays Ltd, St Ives plc

MIX
Paper from
responsible sources
FSC **FSC™ C007454**
www.fsc.org

FSC™ is a non-profit international organisation established to promote
the responsible management of the world's forests. Products carrying the
FSC label are independently certified to assure consumers that they come
from forests that are managed to meet the social, economic and
ecological needs of present and future generations,
and other controlled sources.

Find out more about HarperCollins and the environment at
www.harpercollins.co.uk/green

Contents

Chapter One

MARMALADE DAY

IT WAS A warm summer's day in Darkest Peru and deep in the rainforest, a scruffy bear cub was sitting in the fork of an orange tree sniffing the fruit. He picked one, squeezed it and his furry face split into a huge smile; the oranges were ripe! He'd been waiting for this moment for months. He hurried back to the tree house to tell his relatives the good news.

When he arrived, Aunt Lucy and Uncle Pastuzo

were listening to a crackly recording of *A Friendly Guide to London Life* on their old wind-up gramophone.

It was one of many gifts given to them by a gentleman explorer many years ago; the first person to discover them living in the wild. Now, Aunt Lucy flicked a duster over his photograph.

"You pass a stranger on the street," said the gramophone. "What do you say?"

"Good morning," answered Aunt Lucy. "And then I comment on the weather."

She knew it off by heart and while most of the advice seemed somewhat strange, if they ever visited the explorer in London as he had asked them to, they would need to know how to behave. The record ended with its usual tip,

"And don't forget to raise your hat!"

Uncle Pastuzo raised the explorer's old, tattered, red bush hat that he now wore, picked a grub out of his fur and ate it.

"Very sophisticated," said Aunt Lucy.

"I try my best," he said.

Just then, their young nephew burst into the tree house waving an orange.

"Good morning, my little hurricane," said Aunt Lucy.

"Guess what, Aunt Lucy?" he whooped, skidding across the floor and crashing into the gramophone. He landed on his bottom and as the needle bounced across the record, the gramophone trumpet fell over his head like a helmet.

Uncle Pastuzo grabbed hold of it and pulled, but all this did was lift the cub off the floor with the trumpet still wedged over his ears. He hung in space for a few seconds, then wriggling free, he thrust the orange under his uncle's nose.

"Uncle Pastuzo? They're ripe!"

The cub tore the orange open and the scent of the juice filled the old bear's nostrils.

"Marmalade Day!" he beamed, tumbling over his nephew as they raced each other out of the tree house.

"My favourite time of year," smiled Aunt Lucy, watching Pastuzo swing the cub onto his broad shoulders and carry him off through the trees. The young bear took his uncle's hat and waved it at her.

"Meet you by the marmalade machine, Aunt Lucy!"

"Wash your paws and no licking the ladle," she called, lowering herself sedately into the bamboo stair lift that Pastuzo had rigged up to save her tired old legs.

She watched fondly as they romped off to gather oranges. Ever since the explorer had introduced them to marmalade all those years ago, making it had become an annual ritual. In fact, marmalade had become their favourite food, and Pastuzo had even built an ingenious contraption which helped them produce enough of the sweet preserve to last throughout the year, plus a few extra jars for emergencies.

After she'd adopted her nephew, Aunt Lucy felt it was her duty to pass the marmalade-making skills on to him. It was true that letting a young bear loose with a sticky spoon was asking for trouble, but he seemed to be getting the hang of it.

By the time she reached the forest clearing where the magnificent machine stood, the oranges had been gathered and firewood was already piled up under the huge cooking pot waiting to be lit. Aunt Lucy struck a match.

"It's a bumper crop," said Pastuzo, mounting the rickety wooden bicycle that operated the works.

"This is going to be the best marmalade ever!" said the cub, lobbing the fruit into a funnel. "What did you eat before you discovered marmalade, Uncle Pastuzo?"

"Before the explorer came?" he puffed. "Those

were dark days. We lived like animals, but now we are *civilised!*" He raised his backside to give it a good scratch. "We have marmalade, the most nutritious food known to Bear!"

Aunt Lucy took a wooden spoon from the explorer's old leather boot, which she used as a utensil holder, and stirred the pot.

"All the vitamins and minerals you need for a whole day are contained in just one sandwich," announced Pastuzo as the cub climbed up the nearest tree to pick a fat juicy orange that he'd missed earlier – it was just out of reach.

"One sandwich, Uncle?" he said, stretching as hard as he could to grab the fruit. "Then why do you eat so many?"

Pastuzo patted his stomach apologetically.

"Because they are, unfortunately, *d*elicious!"

The cub managed to catch hold of the fruit he was reaching for, but as he did, he slipped off his branch and hung there, dangling on the stalk, clinging to the orange by both paws. Unaware that he was spinning slowly above her, Aunt Lucy tasted the mixture.

"Mmm… not bad. But it needs something to give it a kick…"

The orange stalk snapped. With a startled cry, the

cub plummeted. Catching his foot on a vine, he swooped across the clearing and, unable to stop himself, knocked the explorer's boot into the pot. It landed with a sticky plop.

"Oh for goodness sake," said Aunt Lucy as he whistled back past her ears.

Trying to slow himself down, he made a grab at his uncle who was peering into the marmalade, but only managed to snatch his hat. He swung back over the cooking pot and, flailing wildly, scooped it to the brim with boiling marmalade.

"You can't be trusted with anything!" said Uncle Pastuzo as the boot bobbed about in the marmalade. "We're going to have to start all over again now."

Just then, the vine snapped, dumping the cub in the long grass. He hid the hat behind his back, hoping to empty it before anyone noticed.

"Give that to me," said his uncle.

"But… but…" stammered the cub.

"No buts!"

Pastuzo grabbed the hat and put it on with a grand flourish, saying, "It's about time I got a bit of respect around here."

Warm marmalade chunks slid down his cheeks. His expression changed.

"Embarrassing… but better than ever!" grinned Uncle Pastuzo.

Aunt Lucy dipped her spoon in the pot. The marmalade tasted even better than last year.

"When I said it needed a kick, this wasn't *quite* what I had in mind," she said, pulling the boot out by its lace. "But it seems to have done the trick!"

By evening, all the jars had been filled… and several of them emptied again. The floor was covered in crusts and crumbs and just one marmalade sandwich remained. The cub lay in a tree branch and gazed at it longingly while his relatives dozed in their hammocks.

"Delicious," burped Uncle Pastuzo.

"Next year we'll try two boots," yawned Aunt Lucy.

The cub sat up.

"Please may I have the last sandwich?"

Uncle Pastuzo opened one eye.

"No, no. A wise bear always keeps a marmalade sandwich under his hat for emergencies," he said, feeling for the last one with his paw and tucking it under his brim. The cub was about to ask what kind of emergency when a deep rumble rattled the marmalade jars.

At first he thought it was Aunt Lucy snoring but as the noise grew louder, the house began to shake. In the far distance, he could see the trees whipping backwards and forwards violently in the wind.

"Aunt Lucy?" he panicked.

She sat up with a start.

"Earthquake!" she exclaimed, reaching for her glasses.

"Get to the shelter!" cried Uncle Pastuzo.

Branches hurtled through the air as Aunt Lucy made a beeline for the stair lift.

"No, too dangerous," said Pastuzo. "You'll have to climb down, old girl."

She looked at him in dismay. It had been years since she'd last climbed down. She gripped the tree trunk and froze.

"Come on, Auntie! I'll catch you," called the cub, scrambling to the bottom.

"Keep going," said Pastuzo, looking over his shoulder at the rapidly approaching quake as Lucy inched her way down. Finally, she made it to the ground and, pelted with twigs and fruit, the three of them ran through the forest trying to dodge the obstacles thrown into their path.

"Nearly there, Aunt Lucy!" yelled the cub over the screaming wind. She was lagging behind. Trying desperately to put a spurt on, she tripped and fell. There was an ear-splitting creak as a huge tree keeled over towards her.

"Look out, Auntie!" shouted the cub.

Pastuzo raced forward to catch it by the trunk, but nothing could have stopped it. It landed on top of Aunt Lucy, pinning her down by the leg. She let out a sharp cry. The cub knelt down beside her.

"Don't worry, Aunt Lucy. We'll soon have you out."

"Keep going before we all get killed!" she said urgently. "Pastuzo, take him with you."

The old bear shook his head. "I'm going nowhere without you."

Using every ounce of his strength, he managed to lift the tree trunk just enough for her to pull her leg out.

"Lean on me, Aunt Lucy," said the cub. "I might not be very tall but I *am* very strong. It must be all the vitamins and minerals in the marmalade."

Aunt Lucy smiled weakly and, allowing herself

to be pulled up, she hobbled towards the shelter as fast as she could, using her nephew as a crutch.

"Don't look back, darling," she said. "Whatever you do, don't look back."

It was only once inside the shelter with Aunt Lucy that the little cub realised his uncle was no longer with them.

"Uncle Pastuzo?" he wailed. "Uncle... where are you?"

He pushed open the door to go and look for him but Aunt Lucy hauled him back inside.

"Get down!" she cried, as another tree splintered and fell towards the shelter. There was a thunderous crash, then everything went black.

Chapter Two

BEAR ABOARD

DAWN CAME. THE earthquake had passed. The forest was eerily silent, as if the birds had lost the will to sing. A parrot sat mournfully in the uprooted tree which had landed against the bears' shelter. Just then, the branch it was sitting on jerked. The parrot screeched and flew off as Aunt Lucy emerged slowly.

The cub stepped out of the shelter and blinked in the sunlight. He gazed in disbelief at all the fallen trees. He hardly recognised the place.

"Oh, Aunt Lucy," he sighed. "I hope that earthquake hasn't broken our marmalade jars. Uncle Pastuzo will be furious."

"Let's go home and see if he's there," said Aunt Lucy quietly, limping off.

"Of course he's there," said the cub. "He'll be mending our tree house."

But when they arrived, there was no uncle and no tree house to mend. It had been ripped out by the earthquake and dashed to the floor in a thousand pieces.

"Pastuzo?" called Aunt Lucy fearfully. "Past...u... zo! Please be somewhere safe."

They picked their way through the pile of twisted timber that had once been their home, throwing aside the broken jars, crushed kettle and smashed gramophone as they searched frantically under the fallen branches for him. The cub began to dig furiously with his paws.

"Uncle Pastuzo...? Uncle Pastuz... *Oh!*"

Aunt Lucy looked up and stumbled over the rubble towards him.

"What is it? Have you found him?"

The cub gave a mournful sob and held up a hat with marmalade stains under the brim. It was all that remained of Uncle Pastuzo. Aunt Lucy's face crumpled. She took the hat and clung to the cub in the middle of the flattened forest.

"What are we going to do, Aunt Lucy?" he sobbed. "Where shall we go?"

There was nothing left for them here. She bent down stiffly and picked up a snow globe that was lying in the dirt. It was a gift from the explorer and a miracle that it had survived. She gave it a shake. As the snowflakes fell on the miniature model of Buckingham Palace, Aunt Lucy said slowly,

"There will always be a welcome in London."

If Aunt Lucy was honest, the Amazon River was a lot longer than she'd thought. After several days in a dug-out canoe crammed with marmalade jars and luggage filled with their few remaining possessions, tempers were getting a little frayed.

"Are we nearly there yet?" asked her nephew for the umpteenth time as they shot over the rapids.

"If I'd known Lima was this far away, I'd have caught the bus," muttered Aunt Lucy, using the explorer's old cricket bat as an oar.

Sharks, shipwrecks and seawater aside, they finally arrived at Lima under cover of darkness. There was a vast container ship being loaded at the docks, bound for Britain. Sneaking up the steps to the harbour, they hid behind a stack of crates and watched as a crane hoisted its cargo on board.

"Let me get this right, Aunt Lucy," said her nephew. "We sit on that crate, the crane picks it up, swings us high into the air and drops us on that big boat?"

Aunt Lucy was beginning to regret she'd suggested it. She'd never been higher than the top of a tree and the thought of it gave her indigestion.

"I'm afraid it's the only way," she said, rubbing her injured leg.

If anyone had looked up at the sky that night, they'd have been amazed to see two bears swinging on a crate among the stars.

"Look at the view, Aunt Lucy. Isn't it wonderful?"

"Splendid," she muttered, her eyes squeezed tightly shut.

She refused to open them again until they landed with a bump on the deck of the ship. Breathing a sigh of relief, she climbed off the crate, staggering under the weight of the brown suitcase she'd packed with marmalade and mementoes for her nephew. He took it and looked concerned.

"Is your leg very bad, Aunt Lucy?"

"I'll be fine," she said, ushering him towards a lifeboat. "In you get."

She lifted the tarpaulin and he threw in his suitcase and clambered inside. He held out his paw to help her onboard, but for some reason she was reluctant to take it.

"Don't worry, Aunt Lucy. It's roomier than it looks under here," he said.

She stood there awkwardly and when she finally spoke, her voice seemed far away.

"Stay out of sight until you get to London, dear."

"But aren't you coming?" laughed the cub.

"It's too far," said Aunt Lucy. "My legs won't make it. I'm too old."

His smile faded.

"But where will you go?"

"Don't you worry about me. There is a lovely home for retired bears in Lima."

The cub swung one leg out of the lifeboat.

"I'll come with you."

Aunt Lucy patted his paw.

"No, you're too young to retire. You have your whole life ahead of you."

The cub stared sadly at his feet. Since his parents had died, Aunt Lucy had always been there for him. And Uncle Pastuzo. They were his family. His world.

"I want to go home," he said.

Aunt Lucy whipped out her hanky and wiped a shred of marmalade off his whiskers.

"Our home is gone. You must find a new one. In London."

He took the handkerchief and blew his nose loudly.

"But I don't know anyone there."

Aunt Lucy took out a luggage label, tied it carefully round his neck and wrote on it in her best handwriting: "Please look after this bear. Thank you."

The cub held out his paws.

"What if nobody does?"

"They will," said Aunt Lucy. "The explorer told us there was once a war in his country. Thousands of children were sent to safety, left at railway stations with labels round their necks. Unknown families took them in and loved them like their own."

"But I'm a bear," said the cub.

"No matter, they won't have forgotten how to treat a stranger," said Aunt Lucy, rummaging for something in her bag.

"Remember the three rules the explorer gave us for living in London: always say hello, talk about the weather and…?"

"Always wear a hat," he said.

She pulled out Uncle Pastuzo's hat, placed it solemnly on his head and kissed his nose.

"Take care, my darling. Be safe."

Someone was coming. He ducked down, pulled the tarpaulin over his head and watched through the holes in the eyelets until Aunt Lucy disappeared into the shadows. Using his suitcase as a pillow, he lay down in the bottom of the lifeboat and, all alone in the world, he wished himself goodnight.

By the time the ship sounded its horn and set sail for England, the little bear was fast asleep.

Several weeks later, the ship arrived at Bristol Docks – and just in time. The cub's lifeboat was littered with empty marmalade jars, and he had almost run out of food. However, in the spirit of the brave explorer he'd heard so much about, he had decided to stop feeling sorry for himself.

Although he missed his aunt and uncle dreadfully, he was determined to make the most of his adventure.

The journey across the ocean had been a long one. Unable to wander on deck for fear of being seen, he had amused himself by peeking out of the lifeboat and noting his observations in the scrapbook Aunt Lucy had given him. This included weather conditions, the sighting of an albatross and the time he'd almost been sick in his hat when the ship rounded the Cape of Good Hope. He'd promised to write to Aunt Lucy when he got to London and this way, he would remember the highlights.

He'd found some interesting seaweed in the bottom of the lifeboat and was just sticking it into the scrapbook with a blob of marmalade when there was a loud parp which made him almost jump out of his fur. At first, he thought the noise must have come from him and wafted his tail. It was only when he spotted dry land that he realised it was the ship's horn announcing that it was about to dock.

As the crew unloaded the cargo, he shut his scrapbook in his suitcase and crept out of the lifeboat.

Keeping a low profile, he pulled his hat down over his eyes and sidled hastily along the ship towards the gangplank.

He was sneaking past a pile of mail sacks when a shadow appeared around the corner and he almost bumped into a dockworker. Seeing a stowaway bear, the man yelped and dropped his clipboard, but by the time he'd gathered all his papers, the bear had vanished. He grabbed an oar and, holding it like a bayonet, began to search for it.

Hiding in a mail sack, the cub peered through the holes in the hessian. He watched as the man got down on his hands and knees and followed a trail of sticky paw prints back to the lifeboat. Using the end of the oar, he flipped back the tarpaulin. There was no bear inside – just a load of empty jars. The man sniffed them. They seemed to smell of... marmalade?

He re-traced his steps and, spotting a pile of mail bags, he tiptoed over. He was just about to search them, when another docker grabbed the sack with the cub in and tossed it over the side of the ship to a man who was loading them on to a mail van.

The driver started the engine. When he thought

it must be safe, the cub opened the sack to stretch his legs. He was hoping to get his first view of the English countryside, but unfortunately, there were no windows in the van. He couldn't tell if it was night or day, but it definitely felt like tea time. Reaching under his hat, he found his last emergency marmalade sandwich, took a bite and, saving the rest for later, snuggled back down in the sack.

A few hours later he woke to the sound of the van doors opening. The sack he was in was loaded onto a trolley along with the rest of the mail. As a porter pushed it along, a voice came over the tannoy:

"The next train from Paddington will be the 8.35 to Plymouth."

The trolley came to a halt, while the porter chatted to a guard. Unseen by either of them, one of the mailbags jumped off and shuffled behind a kiosk. Seconds later, the little bear stepped out of the sack, eyes wide with amazement. So *this* was London! He had read the guides, pored over postcards and played with a pop-up book but this was beyond his wildest expectations. He sat on his suitcase and tried to take it all in; the hustle and bustle, the roar of the trains, the smell of the coffee.

Remembering the first rule for visitors, he stood up and went to say hello to everyone, only to be swept along by a wave of commuters charging towards platform six. He lifted his hat politely and introduced himself to the throng.

"Um… Good evening… Hello? Tipping it down, isn't it?"

To his dismay, no one replied. They were too busy going about their business.

Being a determined bear, he tried again, only to have his hat knocked out of his paw. He crawled after it, buffeted by briefcases as it was kicked along by a sea of feet.

"Excuse me… ouch! Sorry, my hat… oof!… just hit your shoe?"

He was about to get trodden underfoot when he managed to grab his hat and leap aside. He'd always been told that Londoners were friendly and was beginning to wonder if he'd come to the right place.

"Hello? Excuse me, does anyone know where I can find a home… Anyone?"

Disappointed and bewildered, he made his way

over to a sign marked Lost and Found, sat on his suitcase and waited patiently for someone to rescue him.

The clock ticked by and a tannoy announced that any unattended baggage would be taken away and destroyed. It felt like a very long wait.

Chapter Three

PLEASE LOOK AFTER THIS BEAR

RUSH HOUR WAS over and still no one had made the bear feel the slightest bit welcome. Thinking that some marmalade might cheer him up, he took the remains of his sandwich out of his hat. He was about to eat it when a pigeon landed at his side, stared at it hungrily and cooed.

"Sorry, I'm afraid it's all I've got," explained the cub. "It's for emergencies."

The pigeon cooed again. Reluctantly, he threw it a small piece of crust.

"Go on then," he sighed.

The pigeon gobbled it up. Then it waddled back towards him, cocking its head expectantly. The cub waved his sandwich to shoo it away.

"That's quite enough vitamins and minerals for someone your size. Now you're just being greedy."

The pigeon snatched the bread in its beak. As the bear tried to grab it back, a train pulled into Platform 5 and a family got off, bickering with each other.

"Dad, that was the worst 'Fun Wednesday' ever," sulked Jonathan, "I told you we should have gone to the Science Museum."

"Nerd," muttered his sister, Judy.

"Well, I'm sorry you all feel like that," tutted Mr Brown, "but it was my week to choose and personally, I enjoyed the Victorian Wool Museum."

"At least we spent some time together as a family," said Mrs Brown, trying to smooth things over.

"And we learned a lot about wool," added Mr Brown. "Who can name the twelve main types? There's Angora, Cashmere, Merino…"

Jonathan leapt onto a bench and ran along it.

"Yeah, really useful if I'm gonna be an astronaut, Dad."

His father winced.

"You're not 'gonna' be an astronaut…"

"You can be anything you like, Peanut," said Mrs Brown cheerfully as Jonathan launched himself off the end.

"5-4-3-2-1-Blast Off!"

"Don't jump like that, Jonathan," said Mr Brown. "Seven per cent of childhood injuries start with jumping."

"He's only playing, Henry," insisted Mrs Brown, ruffling her daughter's hair. "Did you have fun, Pumpkin?"

Judy – who was listening to "Let's Learn Chinese" through her headphones – cursed her mother in Mandarin.

"It's not Pumpkin, it's *Judy*! And it was *fine* until you jumped in the lake."

Mrs Brown laughed it off.

"It was a Victorian Bathing Pond, darling. It's what you're supposed to do."

"Not naked!" wailed Judy.

Mr Brown was about to tell them the percentage of people who drowned in ponds when he was distracted by a strange creature trying to chase a pigeon away with a hat. Thinking that it might be vicious, he tried to herd his family to safety.

"Stranger Danger! Keep your eyes down."

"What's wrong now?" said Mrs Brown exasperatedly.

He lowered his voice.

"There's some sort of bear over there. Probably selling something. Don't make eye contact or we'll never get rid of it."

"Good evening," said the bear, raising his hat to reveal a pigeon on his head.

"No, thank you," said Mr Brown bluntly.

Jonathan stared at it in astonishment.

"Did that bear just speak?"

"Keep walking," said Mr Brown.

Touched by the forlorn look on the bear's face, Mrs Brown crouched down and gave him a sympathetic smile. Mr Brown turned, aghast.

"Ignore him, Mary!"

"Just a minute, Henry… Hello there, little bear."

"Oh, hello!" he said. "It's coming down in stair rods, isn't it?"

Mrs Brown looked up at the rain beating down on the station roof.

"Stair rods? Yes, that's one way of putting it."

Judy curled her toes in embarrassment.

"Mum! Talking to a bear? You're showing us up."

Mrs Brown took no notice. The bear looked very young and she didn't like to think of it sitting there all alone.

"What's wrong?" she asked.

"It's just… I've been trying to find a home all day," he said wearily. "And you're the first person who's stopped."

Mrs Brown looked round, half-expecting to see a pair of adult bears searching anxiously for him on Paddington Station.

"Find a home? What do you mean? Where are your parents?"

The bear frowned.

"They died when I was small."

"Oh, here we go," interrupted Mr Brown. "Don't believe a word of it, Mary. He's just after your purse."

The bear gave Henry a hard stare. It wasn't as hard as the one Aunt Lucy had taught him but it was the best he could do on an empty stomach.

"Don't upset him, Henry," said Mrs Brown, keen to coax the story out of the bear. "You were saying?"

The bear stopped staring at Mr Brown and continued.

"All I have now is my aunt."

Judy whipped out her mobile.

"What's her number? I'll text her to come and fetch you."

The bear shook his head.

"She doesn't have a number. Even if she did, she can't fetch me. She lives in a home for retired bears in Lima."

"Of course she does," snorted Henry. "Keep back, Jonathan."

Ignoring his father's wishes, Jonathan dashed forward.

"How did you get here?"

The bear straightened his whiskers.

"I stowed away in a lifeboat."

"Cool!" said Jonathan.

"And I ate marmalade. Bears like marmalade."

Jonathan was seriously impressed.

"I didn't know bears could talk."

The cub nodded.

"I'm a very rare sort."

Mary looked at the label round his neck and read it aloud.

"Please look after this bear. Thank you."

She gazed up at Henry who turned away. He'd seen that look before and if he wasn't careful, he was afraid he might cave in.

"No, Mary. He's not our responsibility."

"What are you going to do now?" she asked the bear.

He shrugged.

"I suppose I'll just... sleep here? Still, mustn't grumble."

"That's the spirit. Goodbye," said Henry, chivvying the children along the station. But the bear looked so lonely, Mrs Brown couldn't leave.

"Why don't we find you some help?" she said.

The bear's big, brown eyes lit up.

"Oh, yes please!"

"Stay there," said Mary, "Mr Brown will look after you while we find someone in charge."

Henry folded his arms.

"Oh, *will* Mr Brown!"

"Take him for tea and a bun or something," said Mary, heading off with Jonathan and Judy towards the Information Desk.

"Tea... and... a... bun," mouthed Henry.

"As long as it's no trouble," said the bear.

Henry forced a smile.

"Trouble? No, not at all."

The bear raised his hat politely.

"After you, Mr Brown."

Having bought tea for two and a large cream cake, Mr Brown sat in the booth opposite the bear. He watched uncomfortably as it crammed its cheeks with sugar cubes and drank from the milk jug.

"So… Bear… what's your name?" he said, feeling he ought to make conversation.

Drinking straight from the teapot spout the bear swallowed hard.

"My name is Grrrngk," he answered, spraying Henry with scalding Earl Grey.

"I beg your pardon?"

"Grrrngk," repeated the bear.

"Right," said Mr Brown, staring out of the window.

"You have to say it in the back of your throat," explained the bear.

"I don't have to do anything of the sort," said Mr Brown, but the bear looked so offended, Henry waited until the waitress was out of earshot and gave his best growl.

To his surprise, the bear clapped his paws over his ears and fell off his chair.

"Mr Brown!" he whispered. "What you just said was *extremely* rude!"

As he pulled himself back up, he spotted the rest of the Brown family heading towards the café and clambered onto the table to give them a wave.

"We're back!" called Jonathan.

"At last," grumbled Mr Brown. "Is someone coming to get him?"

Mrs Brown shook her head.

"Everyone's gone for the night. He'll have to come home with us."

The bear took a step back into his tea cup and, to Jonathan's amusement, began hopping about trying to prise it off his foot.

"No way, Mary," said Mr Brown. "Stay there, Jonathan."

"I was only going to help him," protested Jonathan as the bear finally managed to remove the teacup, fell backwards and sat on the cake.

"Good for you, Jonty," said Mrs Brown. "We can't just leave him here."

"*Jonty?*" cringed Judy. "It's Jonathan… Gross! *Now* look what it's doing."

The Browns watched as the cub licked cake out of his hat. He had cream up to his eyebrows and even Mr Brown had to admit he didn't look very threatening.

"All the same, he's not our responsibility," he said.

"He's a young bear who needs our help," said Mrs Brown. "It's only for one night 'til we find the right people to look after him. How much trouble can he be?"

Realising that he was fighting a losing battle, Mr Brown gave in.

"One night only," he said.

"Yes!" said Jonathan.

"Great," groaned Judy. "Having you as a brother is bad enough. Now I have to put up with a bear?"

Mrs Brown helped the cub down from the table. He was so pleased to be rescued, he couldn't stop thanking her.

"You're welcome," she smiled. "Sorry, I don't actually know your name."

He looked sideways at Mr Brown.

"I've got a bear's name," he said. "It's… very hard to pronounce."

"Oh. Well – would you like an English name?" asked Mrs Brown.

The bear looked thoughtful.

"An English name... Like what?"

"Don't give him a stupid one like you keep giving us," said Judy.

"Shush, I'm thinking, Twinkle Toes," said Mrs Brown.

She often made up names for the characters in the books she illustrated, but nothing she could think of suited the bear. It was only when she saw the sign behind him that it came to her.

"Oh look, Henry, it's perfect!"

Mr Brown pulled a face.

"You want to call him Ketchup... Ketchup the Bear?"

"No, *Paddington*."

The bear tried his new name out for size.

"Paddington... Pad-ding-ton... PADDINGTON! I like it!"

"Well then, Paddington," said Mrs Brown. "How would you like to come home with us?"

Paddington beamed from ear to ear. Climbing into a taxi along with the Browns, he told himself that Aunt Lucy had been right; Londoners hadn't forgotten how to treat a stranger. The city lights dazzled him as he pressed his nose to the window.

Jonathan pointed out all the famous landmarks and the lilting rhythm of a Calypso Band filled the air. Paddington Bear decided that London was the place for him.

Little did he know what dangers lurked in the city. As the cab drove past the Natural History Museum in South Kensington, a light glowed from one of the top floor windows – someone was working late. In her office, the Director of Taxidermy was busy sharpening a knife when there came a timid knock at her door.

"Madam Director?"

"Yes, what is it?" she said irritably. "Come in."

A man entered, holding a cage covered with a cloth. Smiling nervously, he made his way gingerly across the room, weaving his way amongst the stuffed animals.

"Another delivery from the docks?" asked Millicent. "Bring it through."

Beckoning him to follow, she poked a stuffed rhino on the nose and a hidden door swung open. They entered the secret stuffing room and she patted the worktable.

"Put it there."

The man put the cage down. Millicent pulled

off the cloth and, seeing an exotic monkey inside, her eyes glittered darkly.

"Mmm!" she said, tickling it under the chin. "You're going to make a fantastic addition to the collection… pass me that syringe, Grant."

The dockworker looked at the cowering monkey and hesitated.

"Won't people ask questions?"

Millicent gave him a withering look, pushed him aside and snatched up the syringe.

"As far as the tree-huggers who run this place are concerned, I wouldn't dream of stuffing a poor defenceless animal," she said. "*But* if I happen to stumble across an old specimen that has been 'lost' in the archives? Well, that's a whole different story."

She smiled to herself and held her needle over the monkey. Grant quickly interrupted.

"There was a weird animal at the docks today. I was doing my rounds when I trod in sticky paw prints. Whatever made them must have stowed away in a lifeboat all the way from Peru. Seems it lived on nothing but marmalade."

Millicent gasped. She dropped the monkey back into the cage.

"Did you say… *marmalade*? What happened to the creature?"

"It sneaked out in the mail van. I tracked it as far as Paddington station." Millicent clapped her hands.

"Excellent! And then?"

"I lost it, Madam Director."

She slapped him hard across the face. There was a shocked silence as Grant clutched his stinging cheek.

"I'm sorry," said Millicent. "But that animal means a great deal to me."

"Why, is he endangered?" whined Grant.

Millicent threw her knife at the wall, piercing a photo of an explorer enjoying the company of two friendly bears in Peru.

"Endangered?" she hissed. "He is now!"

Chapter Four

TROUBLE WITH THE
FACILITIES

THE TAXI PULLED up outside 32 Windsor Gardens. Paddington got out and gazed in awe at the Browns' house. Next door, a curtain twitched. Mr Curry, the Browns' neighbour, liked to keep a strict eye on their comings and goings. It would appear that they had brought a bear home, and he was looking forward to complaining about this no end.

Paddington followed the Browns inside their

home. His eyes widened as he took in his new surroundings. He ran his paws over the smooth, cold floor tiles. Somewhere, a radiator gurgled. "Excuse me," he murmured apologetically, moving over to look at a painted blossom tree on the staircase wall. It reminded him of the rainforest and he stood there admiring it for some time.

"It's not my best," said Mrs Brown modestly.

"It's wonderful!" exclaimed Paddington. "I was beginning to think nobody would ever give me a home but this will do *very* nicely. Thank you so much!"

As he went to hang his hat up, Mr and Mrs Brown exchanged glances.

"Er… we're not giving you a home," said Henry.

"It's just for one night," said Judy, pushing past Jonathan. Paddington put his hat back on and frowned.

"When a young person comes to this country, I'm afraid they can't just move in with the first people they meet," said Mrs Brown gently.

"You need a proper guardian," said Mr Brown, disappearing into the kitchen.

Paddington looked confused.

"A guardian?"

"It's a grown-up who takes you into their home and looks after you," explained Mrs Brown.

"Like you?"

"Yes."

"But *not* you?"

Henry came back in to hammer the point home.

"Not us. We don't do that."

"It's normally someone that you know," said Mary.

Paddington's face fell.

"But what if you don't know anyone?"

"Then the authorities will house you in some kind of government facility," said Mr Brown breezily. Jonathan looked at his father in dismay.

"What? You mean an orphanage?"

"No, no, no. Not an orphanage," blustered Henry. "It will be a sort of institution for young... souls whose parents have... sadly passed on."

Paddington didn't like the sound of it much.

"Maybe I could live with the explorer," he said.

"What explorer?" asked Jonathan.

Paddington sat down on the stairs next to him.

"I never met him," he said. "He visited Peru before I was born, but I know he came from London. He told Aunt Lucy there would always be a warm welcome for us here."

Henry grabbed his car keys.

"What's his name? I'll drive you there now."

"Ah," said Paddington, "I'm afraid I can't tell you that, Mr Brown."

"Why, is it a state secret?" he said.

Paddington felt one of his hard stares coming on.

"He told Aunt Lucy his name but it was hard to pronounce, so we only ever called him *Raghhhhh*," he growled.

Mr Brown threw his keys back in the fruit bowl. Seeing the look on Paddington's face, Mrs Brown tried to stay positive.

"There can't be many explorers who went to Darkest Peru," she said. "Maybe we can find him."

"Without a name? I wouldn't get your hopes up," said Mr Brown, tapping his watch at Jonathan. "Right, you. Come on. Pyjamas."

Jonathan protested, then pounded up the stairs.

"Walk!" bellowed Mr Brown, picking up the phone to his insurance company for a quote on keeping bears overnight.

"Don't worry, Paddington," said Mrs Brown. "I'm sure we can find your explorer. I'll look in my encyclopaedia while you use the facilities."

"The *facilities*?" said Paddington. "I've never used those before, Mrs Brown."

"I thought you might like to freshen up," she

said, noticing the blobs of cake cream encrusting his fur. "Most people do after a long journey."

"Well, if that's what most people do, so shall I," he said, determined to fit in.

"Top of the stairs," said Mrs Brown.

Paddington climbed up the banisters.

"Oh. You're going that way." She smiled. "Mind you don't fall."

"Don't worry about me, Mrs Brown," he said. "Bears are used to climbing."

Unfortunately, bears were *not* used to bathrooms, as Paddington was about to demonstrate. Having doffed his hat at the toilet roll doll, he spotted a pair of toothbrushes in a mug. Giving them a quick sniff, he shoved them in his ears, whirled them round and was astonished to see what came out. Mistaking the big blob of wax for a marmalade chunk, he licked it. Disgusting! Spitting it out, he grabbed a bottle of extra-strong mouthwash and glugged it down. Now his tongue was on fire!

Fanning his mouth with his hat, Paddington knelt down by the toilet bowl to rinse his mouth out when the seat fell over his head. Reaching blindly to pull himself up, he yanked the toilet chain. Water flushed in his face, and he jerked back, snapping the hinges off the seat which was now hanging round his neck like a huge wooden collar.

As he lifted it off, he nudged the toilet roll doll with his elbow. Hearing a splash, he whipped round to see her whirling round in the bowl and before he could grab her, she disappeared down the u-bend, causing a blockage. Paddington watched in horror as the water rose and began to cascade over the toilet rim.

Down below, old Mrs Bird, a relative of the Browns who lived with them, came bustling into the kitchen.

"Batten down the hatches," she said. "There'll be a storm tonight." Her husband had been a sea-going man, and she had a nautical turn of phrase.

Mrs Brown looked up from her encyclopaedia.

"The radio said the weather was clearing up."

"The radio?" snorted Mrs Bird. "I can feel it in my knees. They never lie."

"True," said Mrs Brown.

Jonathan bounded in, wearing his superhero pyjamas along with a pair of old skates with home-made jet packs tied to the back.

"Are those the same ones you wore when we

had to take you to A&E, Cherub?" asked Mrs Brown.

"Nah – these ones are even faster," said Jonathan. "Guess what, Mrs Bird? We found a bear."

"Oh yes?"

Nothing seemed to faze Mrs Bird.

"A real live bear from Peru."

"That's nice, dear," she said.

"You don't seem very surprised," said Jonathan.

"Ach, I gave up being surprised when they came up with the microwave oven." She looked at the microwave. "I still don't trust you."

Judy swept in to make some hot chocolate.

"Where's Paddington going to sleep, Mum?" asked Jonathan.

"Not in my room. He's a *he*," said Judy.

Jonathan flicked her with a rubber band.

"Tony's a he."

Her face went scarlet.

"Shut up, Jonathan."

"Ooh! Who's Tony?" said Mrs Brown.

Jonathan pulled a face.

"Some boy she's in love with."

It was news to Mrs Brown. Judy rarely spoke to her these days.

"Darling, really? When can I meet him?"

Judy glared at Jonathan.

"See what you've done?" she screamed, chasing him round the room as he taunted her.

"Tony! Tony! Tony!"

"Shut up! Shut up! Shut up!"

Mrs Bird intercepted the mug of hot chocolate and tooted sharply on the ship's whistle she kept in her apron pocket.

"No running on deck! Hot liquid in transit."

"Thank you," said Mrs Brown.

Oblivious to the commotion downstairs, Paddington was having troubles of his own. As the water from the blocked toilet flooded the bathroom, he climbed on top of the cistern to keep dry. He was sitting there thinking what to do next when there was a loud crack and the cistern pulled away from the wall, ripping out the plumbing.

Water gushed out of the pipes, and as Paddington fell into the bath he knocked the tap lever, causing the shower hose to rear up at him like a cobra. Defending himself with the toilet seat and a loo brush, he hooked one of its coils and after an exhausting battle, he managed to pin it down at the plug end and tie a knot in it.

He was about to get out of the bath onto dry land when, to his alarm, he realised it was floating; he was in deep water without a life jacket.

Downstairs, the insurance company had put Mr Brown on hold. It wasn't every day they were asked to quote on keeping bears overnight in a house and they weren't about to give him a quick answer. He walked into the kitchen, where an argument was still raging about who was going to share with Paddington.

"It's ok. He can sleep in my room," said Jonathan.

"That bear is not sleeping in anyone's room," said Mr Brown. "He's going in the attic and I want you all to lock your doors."

"I can't find anything about an English explorer in Peru," sighed Mrs Brown.

Henry rolled his eyes.

"Of course you can't."

"Why not?" said Jonathan.

Mr Brown took a sip from his coffee mug, the phone still clamped to his ear.

"The bear made it up. It's just the sort of sob story your mother falls for."

Mrs Brown snapped the encyclopaedia shut.

"Hang on. That's not fair."

"It so *is* fair, Mum," said Judy. "You literally just brought home a random bear. So embarrassing."

As if to distract them, Mrs Bird started knee-bobbing around the room.

"The storm is upon us," she said ominously.

"You and your knees," groaned Henry. "I work with probabilities all day, Mrs Bird, and I can tell you for a fact it is *not* going to rain indoors!"

Just then, a drop of water plopped into his coffee.

"Thar she blows!" cried Mrs Bird triumphantly.

Henry took one look at the damp stain spreading across the ceiling and ran up the stairs yelling into his phone.

"Yes, that sounds fine. No, don't read me the terms and conditions. I just want to action this as soon as... no, don't put me on hold again!"

By now, the bath was floating in four feet of water. Paddington was steering it round in circles with the toilet brush when Henry shouted through the door.

"What's going on in there?"

"Nothing, Mr Brown. I'm just having a spot of bother with the facilities."

Henry turned the handle, releasing a tidal wave

of water that blasted him against the banisters. He watched in disbelief as Paddington sailed past him in the bath, shot down the stairs and scraped to a halt in the kitchen.

"Lovely weather for ducks!" said Paddington, tipping water out of his hat.

Speechless, Henry surveyed the damage. The insurance company came back on the phone.

"Mr Brown? We now have a quote for you regarding bears…"

"Forget it," he groaned.

"Paddington?" said Jonathan, awestruck. "That was amazing."

That night, Paddington stood on the bed in the attic and drew a picture of London in the condensation on the window. It looked like the one in his pop-up book the explorer had left in Peru, but in reality, London was nothing like he'd imagined; everyone was in such a hurry and no one said hello or wore a hat. Feeling homesick, he filled his fountain pen and, spilling ink on the sheets, began writing a letter to his aunt.

"Dear Aunt Lucy, I have arrived and so far it has rained, poured, tipped, bucketed and chucked it down. The

buildings are very big and the trees are very small and you can no longer turn up at the station and get a home."

Hm – it sounded a bit glum. Paddington tried to put a bright spin on things for Aunt Lucy's sake.

"The Browns are a curious tribe," he wrote. *"They live in separate compartments and shout through the walls. Mr Brown is something called a Risk Analyst and says having a bear in the house increases the chances of fire, flood and pestilence by 400 per cent. Mrs Brown illustrates stories. Her latest is set in the sewers under London but she's stuck because she can't imagine what her hero looks like…"*

Paddington could hear them arguing downstairs.

"The man I married would never have left a young bear shivering on a platform," said Mary.

"I'm not the man you married," said Henry. "I'm a father and it's my job to protect this family. First thing tomorrow, that bear is out of here!"

Paddington gave a deep sigh. He had already grown fond of Jonathan and he was sure his sister was lovely, really. He blotted the letter on the pillowcase and wrote some more.

"Judy finds everyone embarrassing and is learning Chinese so she can run away with her boyfriend and Jonathan wants to be an astronaut but Mr Brown only

lets him play sensible games so he makes up his own dangerous ones. Last year he made a pair of rocket boots but he ended up in hospital and now he is only allowed to play with educational, indoor toys from Mr Brown's childhood.

The family live with an elderly relative called Mrs Bird, whose husband was in the Navy so she likes everything ship-shape."

He was about to tell Aunt Lucy about his trouble with the facilities and how Mrs Bird had fixed the pipes with a welding torch but decided that it was probably best to gloss over that little episode.

"Tomorrow I am being sent to live in something that is not-an-orphanage..."

He chewed his pen anxiously. It didn't sound like the kind of home he was hoping for at all. There was a tap at his door and Mrs Brown came in.

"Can't you sleep, Paddington? Me neither, but I've been thinking. You must know something about this explorer that could help us find him."

Paddington thought about it. "Well. I know he came from London. And I think he must have worn glasses, because he gave Aunt Lucy a pair... and he gave Uncle Pastuzo this hat."

"That's brilliant!" cried Mrs Brown. "My friend,

Mr Gruber, runs an antique shop. He knows a lot about old things like that. I bet he could help us find your explorer."

Paddington almost swallowed his pen lid.

"Oh! But didn't Mr Brown say…"

Mrs Brown plumped the pillows.

"Never mind what Mr Brown said. I'm not standing by while there's a chance of finding you a happy home. Try and get some sleep, ok? Night night."

As she left, Paddington crossed out the last line of his letter and rewrote it:

"Tomorrow I am going to find the explorer. Love Paddington.

PS That is now my name."

He yawned. It had been a long day and he was about to get under the duvet when he changed his mind. Used to sleeping in a tree, he climbed up to the ceiling, bedded down on a wooden beam and closed his eyes.

While Paddington began to dream, something more like a nightmare was unfolding at Paddington station. In the security operating room, a ceiling panel had just been lifted. A tranquilliser gun poked through and fired two darts at the unsuspecting guards. They slumped forward, and a woman lowered herself into the room and started scrolling through the footage on the CCTV monitors.

Seeing Paddington getting into a taxi with the Browns, she zoomed in on the licence plate and noted down the number.

"Gotcha!" said Millicent.

Chapter Five

PAW AND ORDER

As THE SUN rose over Windsor Gardens, Paddington woke to the sound of cooing; the pigeon that had pestered him at the station was watching him through the window. He was about to bang on the glass when a whole flock of them landed on the windowsill. With a startled squeak, Paddington fell off the ceiling beam and on to the floor.

Luckily, he was well-padded, and didn't hurt himself – he was anyway far more concerned about the safety of the marmalade sandwich that Mrs Bird had given him at bedtime. Relieved to see it was still in one piece, he tucked it back under his hat and headed downstairs for breakfast. Passing the bathroom, he saw Henry loading his toothbrush.

"Good morning, Mr Brown," called Paddington cheerfully. "You're not cleaning your teeth with your ear brush, are you?"

It gradually dawned on Henry what Paddington must have used his toothbrush for yesterday. He began spitting violently into the sink. Quite unawares, Paddington jauntily mounted the banisters and slid all the way down.

"Cool!" said Jonathan, swinging his leg over the rail. He was about to slide after Paddington when his father appeared, foaming at the mouth.

"Jonathan! Don't you dare. 34 per cent of pre-breakfast accidents involve banisters."

"But Paddington just…"

Mr Brown folded his arms.

"I don't care what Paddington just…"

Downstairs, Paddington was taking his place at the kitchen table for breakfast with the rest of the household.

"You know all my bathroom stuff has been ruined?" scowled Judy.

Mrs Brown opened a fresh jar of marmalade.

"Well, I don't like you using all those chemicals anyway, Sweet Pea."

Judy slammed the sugar bowl down.

"It's J–U–D–Y. Not Twinkle Toes. Not Sugar Plum. Not Sweet Pea."

Jonathan came in and pretended to hang himself with his school tie.

"Mum, why is Dad so boring and annoying?" he said.

Mr Brown walked in and walked straight out again. It was the same every breakfast time – the arguing, the name-calling. The lack of respect for the head of the household.

"It's for your own good, Jonathan," he shouted from the next room.

"I can't even wash my own face!" moaned Judy.

"Allow me," said Paddington, licking the crumbs off her cheek.

Judy slid so far down her chair, she almost went under the table.

"Gross," she whimpered.

"Ha! In your *face*," said Jonathan, roaring with laughter.

"It's just what bears do in the wild, darling," soothed Mrs Brown. "He wants to be friends."

As if to prove it, Paddington licked Jonathan from nose to chin with a loud slurp.

"That wiped the grin off, didn't it, laddie," said Mrs Bird, chivvying him out of the room. "School ahoy, chop, chop!"

She handed Henry his brief case.

"May the sea be calm," she said.

"I'm not going by sea, Mrs Bird," said Mr Brown tartly. "I'll be catching the tube to the office at 8.25, just as I do every weekday."

"Boring," said Jonathan. "Can Paddington come to school with me?"

Judy threw her hands in the air.

"Do *not* tell your friends we've got a bear! They already think we're weird."

Jonathan forced her to smell his P.E. bag.

"Stop it and no," said Henry. "Your mother's taking Paddington to the er… special place we discussed. You do know where you're going, don't you, Mary?"

"I do, yes," she said, shutting the door behind them.

As Paddington stepped out into the street with the rest of the family, Mr Curry was leaning out of his window with nail scissors, pretending to trim his chives.

"Heck of a racket coming from your way last night, Brown," he said.

Henry gritted his teeth.

"Hello, Mr Curry. Sorry if we disturbed you."

Mr Curry glared at the bear on the pavement and pointed his scissors at him. "Don't believe we've had the pleasure."

"This is Paddington," said Mrs Brown.

Paddington raised his hat.

"Good morning!"

"He's a bear," added Jonathan.

"I can see that," sneered Mr Curry. "You must be a long way from home, Bear."

"Darkest Peru," said Paddington.

Mr Curry looked as if he had a nasty smell under his nose.

"Don't worry, he's not stopping," said Mr Brown.

"Good. I don't want to be kept up by any of your loud jungle music," said Mr Curry, slamming his window shut.

"Take no notice, Paddington," said Mrs Brown. "His bark's worse than his bite."

"He *bites*?"

Paddington made a note to keep well out of Mr Curry's way.

As the Browns arrived at Westbourne Oak underground station, a terrier on a lead got a strong whiff of Bear and started yapping.

"Watch out, Paddington," said Henry. "There are thieves and murderers on every platform. Follow us and do exactly as you're told."

"Righto, Mr Brown," said Paddington, anxious to keep out of trouble after last night's waterworks. He watched as the Browns fed their tickets into a slot in the barrier. However, being on the short side, he didn't see them take it out again from the slot on top. He posted his own ticket, and was about to walk through when the gates clapped shut and sent him flying backwards. A stern-looking ticket inspector opened the barrier and handed him back his ticket.

"Thank you, Officer," said Paddington.

He was so busy raising his hat that by the time he reached the barrier, it had snapped shut again, trapping him by his nose.

"Erb...? Excuse be, Obbicer?" he called.

It wasn't until the Browns reached the bottom of the escalator that they realised he was missing.

"Where's Paddington?" groaned Henry.

"He can't have gone far," said Mrs Brown.

"Shame," muttered Judy.

As the family spread out to look for him, Paddington hovered at the top of the escalator. He was about to step on when he read the sign: *Dogs must be carried.*

Anxious not to break the rules, he crawled back under the ticket barrier to the station entrance and returned moments later with a yappy dog in his arms. Happy that he'd obeyed the instructions to the letter, he rode down the escalator just as Mr Brown was coming up to find him. Henry saw the top of his hat over the handrail and called out.

"Paddington! Over here!"

"Coming, Mr Brown!" said Paddington. He began running up the down escalator and crashed into a business man who was coming the other way. The dog flew out of his arms, and Paddington rolled to the bottom of the escalator. He looked up to find Henry standing over him, holding the dog.

"You should keep that bear on a lead!" said the owner angrily, taking his dog back.

"He's not my bear," insisted Henry.

"I'm my own bear," said Paddington.

Henry handed Mary a laminated sheet. "I've printed you off directions to the authorities," he said.

"Thank you, Henry," replied Mary. "I know exactly where I'm going. It's a lovely day, isn't it, Paddington? Let's walk, shall we?"

"Bye, Paddington," said Jonathan. "I hope the authorities don't do bears and you come home."

"Don't worry," said Paddington cheerfully. "Mrs Brown has a plan."

Paddington hadn't known what to expect of an antiques shop, but he wasn't disappointed. The window was full of fascinating objects, from stuffed crocodiles to clothes mangles. Mary pushed the door open.

"Hello, Mr Gruber. Here we are!"

A twinkly-eyed old man looked up from the dusty book he was consulting and greeted them with open arms.

"Mrs Brown! And you must be the young gentleman whose hat sounds so fascinating? Come in. You're just in time for elevenses."

A clock struck and to Paddington's surprise, a hatch opened in its side and a model steam train emerged with a loud whistle. As it did a circuit round the shop, Mr Gruber patted his horsehair sofa and invited them to sit down. The engine came to a halt beside them, and Mr Gruber reached over and turned a tap on its tank, filling three cups with steaming cocoa.

"Every morning this train arrives at eleven," he said. "Bringing salvation, just like the one I took many years ago…"

He opened the goods van, took out three sticky buns and handed them round. Paddington put a whole one in his mouth.

"Good for you, Mr Brown," chuckled the old man. "As I was saying, there was once much trouble in my country of Hungary, so my parents sent me by train all the way across Europe when I was not much older than you are now."

"Was it hard to find a home?" asked Paddington.

Mr Gruber pressed his fingers together.

"My great aunt took me in. But I soon learned a home is more than the roof over your head. My body travelled fast, but my heart? She took longer to arrive."

The bell over the shop door tinkled. A man in a suit entered and deliberately bumped into a man in a turban who was examining a Victorian bedpan. Making sure no-one was looking, he stole his wallet.

"May I take a look at your hat, Mr Brown?" said Mr Gruber.

"My hat? Oh yes. Thank you," said Paddington.

Mr Gruber turned it over in his hands and a sandwich fell out.

"The lining is a most unusual colour," he murmured. "Hard to say how much is original and how much is marmalade."

"My uncle always kept a sandwich in his hat for emergencies," explained Paddington.

"You are pulling my legs off! How splendid," chortled Mr Gruber, holding his magnifying glass over the hat. "Ooh, I detect the faintest trace of the maker's mark."

The man in the turban left, not realising he'd been robbed. Just then, the man in the suit noticed Paddington staring at him. Assuming the little bear had seen everything, he lost his nerve, dropped the wallet and made a brisk exit. Paddington leapt off the sofa.

"Oh. Where are you going?" asked Mary.

"Gentleman dropped his wallet!" called Paddington, sprinting after the thief.

Convinced that he'd been caught in the act, the pickpocket ran round the corner, dodging pedestrians in the busy market place.

"Excuse me sir…" called Paddington breathlessly. "Just trying to return your lost property!"

Up ahead, a little boy standing with his mum dropped his skateboard. It rolled into Paddington's path, and before he knew it, Paddington had accidentally stood on it and shot straight into a stall of novelty costumes. He sailed out the other side wearing a police helmet and blowing a whistle. The thief jumped into his car and screeched off.

A double-decker bus pulled up alongside Paddington. He reached for the pole on the hop-on platform to follow the car, but missed and instead grabbed the handle of a retractable lead which just happened to belong to the same dog he'd taken down the escalator.

"Not you again!" yelled the owner. "What do you think you're playing at?"

He started attacking Paddington with an umbrella. "Leave my dog alone!"

Trying to avoid the blows, Paddington grabbed hold

of the umbrella. Just then, the bus went over a speed bump and the lead suddenly shot out. With Paddington clinging to its end for dear life, it dragged the little bear past a parked police car like a water skier. Seeing his blue helmet, the officers in the car mistook him for one of their own and went into action.

"Tango Charlie. Officer in distress. Requesting assistance. Go! Go! Go!"

Skiing alongside the bus, Paddington saw a truck hurtling towards him on the other side of the road. Acting fast, he pressed the umbrella button. It whooshed open and he was lifted high into the air. The thief, driving below, caught sight of him in his rear view mirror and his jaw dropped. He was so busy watching Paddington and not the road, he drove straight into a lamp post.

"Don't worry, I've got your wallet, sir!" Paddington called to the dazed crook as he wafted past.

At that very moment, Judy was gazing out of her classroom window during a boring English lesson.

"In *A Winter's Tale*, who can complete Shakespeare's most famous stage direction?" asked the teacher, "Exit pursued by a…?"

"Bear!" yelled Judy, seeing a furry figure sailing past with an umbrella.

"Very good, Judy… Sit *down,* Class 9!" called the teacher, as the rest of the pupils got out of their seats to watch the spectacle. The bus screeched to a halt to avoid the crashed car, and the thief came to his senses again, jumped out of the car and began to run. Just then, Paddington's umbrella turned inside out and, as the pickpocket ran past the school gates, Paddington crash-landed on top of him, sending him sprawling across the pavement.

"You dropped your wallet," puffed Paddington, looking sideways at all the other wallets that had fallen out of the thief's jacket. "Oh! You've got quite a few."

"He certainly has," said a burly police officer, arriving at the scene.

A loud cheer erupted from Judy's classmates. Even she couldn't help joining in and as the thief was driven away, Paddington looked up and saw her.

"Hello, Judy!" he waved.

She shrank back from the window. She was never going to live this down.

"Judy Brown, is that your bear?" said one of the girls. "You're so lucky. My mum won't even let me have a hamster."

"He's awesome," said Tony.

Suddenly, Judy saw Paddington in a whole new light.

"Yep," she said proudly. "That's my bear."

Paddington made his way back through the market, where the stall holders gave him a standing ovation, patting him on the back as he passed.

"There he is, Bear of the moment! Well done, mate!"

When he arrived at the antique shop, Mr Gruber couldn't thank him enough.

"Mr Brown, I owe you many buns!" he said. "That scoundrel has been pock-picketing people round here for many weeks."

"Well done, Paddington," said Mary. "And there's more good news."

"Indeed," said Mr Gruber. "Yours isn't any old hat, Mr Brown. It was made for a member of a famous old explorer's society known as the Geographers' Guild. Go there tomorrow. I bet you my dollar bottom they will tell you who it belonged to."

Paddington couldn't believe his good fortune.

Unfortunately, his luck was about to run out. While Mr Gruber gave him a guided tour of the shop and showed him his collection of priceless Roman marmalade jars, Millicent was up to no good.

She had tracked down the cab driver who had given Paddington and the Browns a lift from the station the night before. Right now, he was hanging upside down by his ankles in a hunter's trap under Charing Cross Bridge.

"I'll ask you one last time," said Millicent, threatening him with a pair of tweezers. "Where did you take that bear?"

"Can't tell you, love," said the man. "It's against the Cabbies' Code."

Millicent yanked out one of his long, black nasal hairs.

"32 Windsor Gardens!" he squealed, clutching his nose.

She cut the rope.

"Thank you," she said. "It's time I paid Ursus Marmalada Junior a little visit."

"I'd avoid the fly-over, love," called the cabbie as he fell into the Thames. "It's murder during rush hour."

Chapter Six

ALL RECORDS DESTROYED

WHEN MR BROWN came home from work, he wasn't best pleased to find that a certain bear was still in his house. He brought it up with Mrs Brown while they were washing-up after dinner, little realising that Paddington was sitting on the stairs listening with Jonathan.

"One night, you said, Mary. You promised to take him to the authorities."

"I never *promised*!"

"Well, you very heavily implied that you would."

"I know, and I'm sorry. But the point is, Paddington was telling the truth. There really *is* an explorer."

Henry threw his tea towel down and gazed up at the ceiling.

"What are you doing?" said Mary.

"I'm doing my looking-away face," he said.

She took him by the shoulders.

"Look at me, Henry. All we have to do is take him to the Geographers' Guild."

He put his hand up.

"Oh. The hand's gone up," said Mrs Brown.

"Stop!" he said. "We've done quite enough for that bear."

"And the voice," she said.

Paddington looked at Jonathan sadly.

"I'd better go, hadn't I? Mr Brown doesn't want me here."

He got up to leave. Jonathan sat him back down.

"Wait – he'll come round. He's just being Dad."

But Mr Brown wasn't about to change his mind.

"That bear is a danger to the family, Mary," he said. "Jonathan's irresponsible enough without any encouragement."

Jonathan was about to protest when Judy came through the front door, waving the local paper.

"Seen this?" she said, squeezing next to Paddington. There was a photo of him on the front page sitting on the thief. Jonathan read the headline.

"*Paw and Order*...Wow, you've only been in London one day and you're already famous!"

Judy gave Paddington a squeeze.

"Sorry if I was horrid before. It's just... it's a new school and I didn't want everyone to think I was weird."

"That's ok," said Paddington. "I don't want everyone to think I am either."

She pressed her ear to the banister.

"What's Dad ranting on about now?" she said as Henry's agitated voice drifted up from the kitchen.

"Mary, that bear put earwax on my toothbrush!"

Realising his mistake, Paddington raised his eyebrows as Jonathan and Judy collapsed in a fit of giggles.

"I'm afraid Mr Brown doesn't find me very amusing," he sighed.

"That's because he's boring," said Jonathan. "He always has been."

Mrs Bird was putting the washing away on the landing and overheard.

"Och!" she said. "He was a very different man when I first knew him."

Judy looked up.

"Did he have a personality transplant, Mrs Bird?"

"No, a motorbike," she said. "1000cc. He was a daredevil back in the day."

"What changed?" asked Jonathan.

Mrs Bird folded Henry's sensible beige trousers and put them on the shelf.

"He became a father," she said. "If he plays things a little safe, it's only because he loves you. He's just put his daring self on hold like most dads. He exchanged the bike for a beige Volvo to take you home from the hospital when you were born, Judy. Safety first."

"So it's all our fault?" said Judy.

Mrs Bird semaphored with a pair of red socks.

"Just give him a chance to show his true colours."

The children sat in silence, stunned by her revelation. Then Judy spoke.

"If anyone could turn Dad around, I bet you could, Paddington."

Paddington wasn't so sure.

"Well, I did try to make a good impression. I always raise my hat."

"At which point, you are technically naked," she said.

He put his hat back on hastily.

"Am I? What should I do?"

Judy and Jonathan took a paw each and led him off to the bathroom.

"Don't worry, Paddington. We'll show you the ropes."

"There are ropes?" he said.

He was wary of the facilities after last night's episode, but he needn't have worried. Being scrubbed from head to toe with bubble bath was a lot more fun than he imagined, especially when he shook himself and soaked them both.

Hearing the children shriek, Henry stopped in mid-argument.

"They're screaming, Mary!" He panicked, racing upstairs.

"No, darling. That's the sound of laughter," she said.

Henry stopped in his tracks; Paddington was in Judy's room with Mrs Bird's pink rollers in his wet fur, being blow-dried.

"Mind you don't singe his fur, Judy," fussed Jonathan.

Henry's face melted into a smile. He watched as Paddington sat in a chair reading a magazine while the children buffed his claws.

"See?" said Mary. "Just playing together. They haven't done that for ages."

Jonathan led Paddington over to the mirror. He looked at his reflection and gasped. His fur was gleaming gold and perfectly bouffant.

"Ah, here it is!" said Mrs Bird, pulling a little coat with a hood out of an old trunk. She bustled into Judy's room and gave it to Paddington.

"My old duffel!" said Jonathan.

"Actually, it was mine first," said Judy.

"Actually… it was mine," said Henry.

The children turned to see their parents standing in the doorway.

"He wore it on his first day to school," said Mary.

"Were you really once a child, Dad?" said Jonathan.

Henry knelt down and helped Paddington do the toggles up.

"I must say it suits you very well," he said.

"Please don't send him to the authorities," begged Jonathan.

Judy stood by her brother.

"You will at least try the Geographers' Guild first, won't you, Dad?"

Henry looked at their hopeful faces and couldn't bring himself to ruin the moment.

"Yes, of course I will."

Jonathan jumped up and down and whooped. "Yes!"

Paddington was glowing and it wasn't just because he'd had a warm shower.

"Thank you very much, Mr Brown," he said.

The next day, Paddington put one of Mrs Bird's best marmalade baguettes under his hat and set off with Henry to the Geographers' Guild. He could hardly wait to find out the name of the explorer. Together, they hurried past the phone box at the corner of Windsor Gardens, without noticing that someone was lurking inside it.

Millicent raised her dart gun. She was just lining it up with the back of Paddington's hat when Mr Curry appeared and rapped on the window.

"Can I help you, son?" he said. "You've been in there for forty-seven minutes. Either that's a very long call or you're placing dodgy adverts in a public place."

Millicent hid the gun in her bag, whipped off her cap and smoothed down her short blonde hair.

"I'm terribly sorry," she purred.

Confronted by a beautiful woman instead of the hooligan he was expecting, Mr Curry's legs turned to jelly.

"Not a problem, young lady," he stammered. "Apologies if I startled you, just doing my neighbourly duty. We've had some very unsavoury characters hanging around lately, not least a bear. Filthy creature, all marmalade and whiskers."

The mere mention of marmalade made Millicent's hackles rise.

"That bear is the reason I'm here," she said, lowering her voice. "We may have something in common."

"Really?" said Mr Curry, unable to imagine what that could possibly be.

"You look like someone I could... trust," cooed Millicent. "Can we talk in private?"

Wishing he'd swept his toenail clippings off the sofa, Mr Curry let her into his flat.

"You have a beautiful home, Mr Curry," purred Millicent, casting her eye over the filthy furniture.

"I can see how having a bear living next door might lower its value."

Mr Curry offered her a bowl of stale nuts and sat beside her on the sagging sofa. "I suppose I should be grateful it's only one bear," he said.

"Oh, it always starts with one," said Millicent. "But before you know it, there's a relative. Then a couple of friends who are 'doing the garden' but never leave. The whole street will be crawling with them. Drains clogged with fur, buns thrown at old ladies. Raucous all-night picnics…"

Mr Curry turned pale.

"My god. But what can we do?"

She sidled up to him and murmured breathily, "I have connections. If I catch the bear, I can have it sent where it belongs, but I can't do it alone. I need a strong, capable man to help me."

Mr Curry scratched his greasy comb-over.

"No one springs to mind."

Millicent batted her eyelashes.

"I mean *you*, Mr Curry. You could easily keep an eye on him… just for me?"

"Of course!" he said eagerly. "I can hear every word that goes on in that house. Sometimes I don't even need to press a glass to the wall."

"Well, you do that and as soon as he's alone, we'll pounce."

She held out her hand.

"Partners?"

Mr Curry gave it a limp, sweaty shake.

"Partners."

He was putty in her hands.

Paddington was most impressed with The Geographers' Guild. It was a grand old building and the receptionist gave them a very warm welcome.

"Good morning, gentlemen. Are you members?" she simpered.

"No," said Henry, "but we're looking for one of your members. I'm afraid we don't have his name but we do know he went on an expedition you funded to Peru."

"*Darkest* Peru," added Paddington.

"Lovely," she said. "Won't keep you a moment."

The receptionist tapped busily on her computer. She found what she was looking for, and a canister emerged from one of the tubes in front of her. She opened it and pulled out a piece of paper. As she read it, her expression changed.

"We've never been to Peru," she snapped.

Paddington couldn't believe his ears.

"But you must have done!"

"I can see you're very busy," said Henry. "Perhaps we could go and check?"

She pursed her lips.

"There are over two million letters, diaries and artefacts in our archive, meticulously filed, and they don't stay that way by letting strange men and their bears go poking around..."

"Now listen!" protested Henry.

The receptionist glared at him over the top of her glasses.

"I'm going to have to ask you to leave," she said sternly.

Henry was about to refuse when he noticed a security guard with enormous biceps on patrol and backed down.

"Come on, Paddington," he grumbled. "Paddington...?"

The little bear was nowhere to be seen. Henry walked towards the exit, calling his name. Suddenly, a familiar voice hissed from a cleaning cupboard just next to him.

"Psst... Mr Brown? I'm here!"

Making sure no one was watching, Mr Brown slipped inside and found Paddington sitting among the mops and buckets.

"What are you doing?" he said.

"We *have* to find a way in," said Paddington.

"Paddington," asked Henry, "please don't take this the wrong way, but are you certain there was an explorer? You didn't just find a hat and make up some…" He trailed to a halt. By now, Paddington had mastered his hard stare – and was unleashing its full force on Henry.

"What… why are you looking at me like that?" said Henry, loosening his collar. "Is it me or is it hot in here? Why do I feel so…?"

"Uncomfortable?" supplied Paddington. "Aunt Lucy taught me to do hard stares when people forget their manners. Mr Brown, I know you're not sure about me—"

"It's not that…" said Henry.

"I know," said Paddington. "When we first met, I wasn't sure about you either. You all argued a lot and your bathroom was a death trap. But now I realise you love each other. You have a wonderful home and, if I can find the explorer, maybe I can have one too. So – I've had an idea, but I need your help."

Mr Brown felt so humbled, he could hardly refuse. Five minutes later, he found himself coming out of an elevator dressed as a cleaning lady pushing a cart.

"This is never going to work," he said, fiddling with his floral headscarf.

"It will. You look very pretty," whispered Paddington, hidden beneath a pile of dusters on the cart...

Henry pushed the cleaning cart towards a large research room divided into work stations. They were occupied by geographers who were busy posting and retrieving documents in canisters via two tubes that led in and out of each cubicle. Henry was about to enter when a sleazy-looking guard on the door gave him a cheeky wink.

"Morning, Gorgeous."

"Oh, hello there," said Henry, adopting a falsetto Welsh accent. He was about to dash past when the guard stopped him.

"Hold up. I haven't seen you before."

"That's right, I only just started," trilled Henry.

"Thought so," flirted the guard. "Lovely day for it."

Henry gulped.

"A real scorcher. Just like you," leered the guard, patting his bottom. "In you go, love."

Henry squealed and scuttled inside. Spotting an empty workstation, he sat down and started typing on the computer.

"Right. Darkest Peru… well, I never… 200 items!"

"I knew that lady was lying," said Paddington, climbing out of the cart.

Henry pressed a button and a canister shot out. He read the message inside.

"All Records Destroyed… I wonder why?"

He was about to check the other canisters when the guard whistled at him.

"Oi! New girl!"

Henry's heart sank.

"Keep your head down, Paddington," he whispered as he went to see what the man wanted.

"Forgot to check your pass, darlin'," leered the guard.

Henry patted the pockets in the overall he was wearing.

"My pass? Right… Ah, this must be it."

He pulled out the one belonging to the woman whose uniform he'd borrowed but to his dismay and relief, he looked nothing like her. She was enormously fat, had a mole the size of a chocolate button, and only one arm.

"Whoa! You've changed a bit," said the guard, looking at him suspiciously.

"I've lost weight," said Henry. "And had my mole lasered."

"Oh," said the guard, looking unconvinced. "And the arm's grown back?"

Henry laughed coquettishly and mimed a false limb.

"It's prosthetic."

"Amazing," said the guard. "Looks almost like the real thing."

He took off his ID badge and gave Henry's forearm a little jab with the pin.

"So you really can't feel a thing?"

"Nope," lied Henry bravely.

The guard pushed the pin all the way in.

"Nothing," said Henry, his eyes smarting with pain.

"Modern technology, eh?" said the guard. "I'm off to the toilet. See you later."

Henry gave him a coy wave then, pulling the pin out with a silent scream, he ducked back into the cubicle, rubbing his arm.

"I'm glad you're back, Mr Brown," said Paddington. "I've found something."

He held up a reel of film marked 'Top Secret'.

"Brilliant!" said Henry. "Let's put all the canisters back and get out of here."

Paddington gave him a helping paw but Henry was in such a hurry, he pushed Mrs Bird's marmalade baguette into one of the tubes by mistake.

There was a strange gurgling noise as it was sucked into the system.

"Mr Brown?" said Paddington. "I think my baguette went down the wrong hole."

"Quick, back in the cart," said Henry, pulling the dusters over Paddington.

As Mr Brown steered Paddington stealthily down the corridor, he could hear the geographers grumbling behind him – the automatic tubes had broken down.

"Something's jamming the system," tutted the receptionist.

"Looks like a baguette," said a geographer. "Is that peanut butter, Albert?"

"Too orange," said the man in the next cubicle. "It's marmalade, old boy."

There was a sudden massive explosion of paper,

fluttering down over the lobby like confetti. Henry and Paddington tried to sneak out through the chaos, but just as Henry thought they'd made a clean get-away, the sleazy guard spotted him.

"Hey! Stop that sexy woman!" he yelled.

Henry tipped the cart over. Paddington spilled out and together they ran for the exit and escaped through the door, careering down the steps like partners in crime.

"That was exciting, wasn't it, Mr Brown?" said Paddington as they caught their breath in the Municipal Gardens.

And as they headed home with the top-secret film, Henry had to agree.

Chapter Seven

PADDINGTON COMES UNSTUCK

THAT EVENING, THE Browns sat in the back of the antique shop with Paddington while Mr Gruber loaded the top-secret film onto his old projector.

"So you actually broke in, Dad?" said Jonathan.

"Sounds incredibly brave," said Mary.

"Well," said Henry, puffing himself up, "there's a time for being 'boring and annoying' and there's a time for being a man."

Paddington leant over confidingly to Judy.

"Mr Brown dressed up as a lady."

Judy's mouth fell open.

"What?"

"Oh look, it's starting," said Mr Brown, attempting to distract her. Mrs Brown gave him a sideways glance.

"Sorry, Henry. You did what?"

"In a dress?" said Jonathan.

"No!" said Henry. "More of a housecoat. Quite liberating actually, Mary."

Mr Gruber cleared his throat and the chattering stopped as the screen filled with a landscape of trees, mountains and waterfalls. A distinguished-looking explorer in a red bush hat entered and spoke to the camera.

"Darkest Peru. A vast, unexplored wilderness of strange plants and exotic animals, many of them unknown to science until now!"

Paddington's eyes widened. He climbed down, walked over to the screen and, full of nostalgia, he pressed his nose against it. There was the tree house and there was a very young Aunt Lucy standing with Uncle Pastuzo, waving.

"Oh dear," said Mary, dabbing her eyes as

Paddington waved back longingly at the only family he had ever known.

"Thank goodness you agreed to help him, Henry," she said.

"Can we go to Peru instead of Cornwall, Dad?" said Jonathan.

"No," said Henry. "Cornwall's lovely, while seventeen per cent of South American fauna is deadly poisonous."

"*Shh,*" hissed Judy, "I'm trying to listen."

Twenty minutes later, the wonders of the Amazon came to an end, with Paddington's aunt and uncle giving the explorer a bear hug.

"And now I, Montgomery Clyde, must leave my new friends and return to my human family," said the explorer's voice-over. In the film he called, "Goodbye, Lucy. Goodbye, Pastuzo. If you ever make it to London, you can be sure of a very..."

"...warm welcome," echoed Paddington as the explorer threw his hat to Uncle Pastuzo and headed back into the jungle. Paddington returned to the sofa.

"Montgomery Clyde! We've got his name!"

"It's a huge step forward," said Mr Brown excitedly. "We'll start looking for him tomorrow morning."

That night, Paddington sat up in bed comforted by the thought that Montgomery Clyde might adopt him as his own. There was just one thing that bothered him; despite all their funny little ways, he had become extremely fond of the Browns. It was going to be hard to say goodbye.

The next day, breakfast at the Browns' household was nothing like it used to be. Instead of the usual arguments, everyone was working towards the same mission.

"Paddington, here are the names and addresses of everyone in London," said Henry, plonking a pile of telephone books on the table. "I suggest you spend the morning noting down all the M. Clydes, then we'll pay them all a visit."

"Thank you, Mr Brown," said Paddington gratefully, as Henry grabbed his briefcase and hustled the children to the door.

"Can't we bunk off school to help Paddington?" said Jonathan.

Normally, Henry would have spouted statistics about the percentage of schoolboys who became drop-outs after missing school just once, but part of him very much wanted to phone the office, pretend he had flu and find the explorer too. Luckily, Mrs Bird answered on his behalf.

"I've made your packed lunches now," she said. "Be off with you."

Mary grabbed her coat.

"Wait for me. I'm going to the library to check the electoral roll."

Paddington was very fond of rolls, especially crusty ones and asked if he could come.

"It's not that sort of roll," explained Mary. "It's a list of people's details. Montgomery Clyde might be on it."

"I'll come with you," said Mrs Bird. "We're almost out of marmalade."

They were about to leave when Henry had second thoughts about leaving Paddington home alone.

"It's only for a couple of hours, Henry," said Mary.

"Don't worry about me, Mr Brown," said Paddington. "I'll be fine."

Henry was more worried about the possible damage to his house – the bathroom had only just been fixed.

"Well, try not to break anything," he said.

"I won't, Mr Brown. Have a nice day."

Paddington settled down with the phone books, happily unaware that Mr Curry had just seen the Browns leave with Mrs Bird and had got straight on the phone to Millicent.

"Honey Pot, this is Fierce Eagle."

There was an uncomfortable silence.

"I beg your pardon?" she said.

"It's Mr Curry. We gave ourselves code names remember?"

On the other end of the line, Millicent pretended to stick two fingers down her throat.

"Of course," she said, smoothly.

"The Furry Menace is home alone," said Mr Curry urgently. "I repeat: the Furry Menace is home alone."

"On my way," she said, rolling her eyes.

By the time Millicent arrived, Mr Curry had glued the few remaining strands of his hair down with a whole pot of Brylcreem and was wearing a moth-eaten dinner jacket with a dead carnation in the button hole.

"I need to get on the roof," said Millicent, pushing past him.

"Yes and after, I wondered if you'd like to celebrate by dining with me?" said Mr Curry. "I've got meat paste sandwiches and pickles. They went off on Tuesday but I've given them a sniff and they should be all right."

"Mr Curry! The roof?" said Millicent.

He took her up to his attic and, climbing up a ladder, he opened the hatch.

"And if you feel all sweaty after wrestling that bear into a cage, you can have a soak in my tub," he said.

"You think of everything," grimaced Millicent, imagining the thick ring of scum round Mr Curry's bath.

"Just one more thing, Honey Pot," he called up as she lifted herself through the hatch in the roof. "This is all… humane, isn't it?"

"Of course, Mr Curry."

Millicent kicked the hatch shut and slipped off her long coat to reveal full hunting gear. Armed with a dart gun and smoke grenades, she stepped over to the Browns' roof and attached an electronic pulley system to their chimney.

Down below, Paddington was far too occupied to notice the goings-on up above. He'd torn the corner off a phone book and, keen to mend it, had found Henry's heavy-duty sellotape dispenser.

Unfortunately, the sticky end got stuck to his fur and as he whirled round to find it, the dispenser let out more tape, wrapping itself round him until he looked as if he'd been mummified.

As he tried to unravel himself, Millicent lowered herself silently into the stairwell on the end of the steel cable, headfirst. Spotting the Browns' telephone in the hallway, she raised a monocular to one eye and read the number on it, then dialled it on her mobile.

It was the perfect lure. Hearing the phone ring, Paddington struggled over to answer it. He was still attached to the dispenser and, stretching the tape to its limit, he strained forward to pick up the receiver. As Millicent took aim and fired, the tape suddenly jerked Paddington backwards. She cursed as the tranquilliser dart missed him by millimetres.

Heaving at the sellotape, Paddington shuffled back towards the phone again. Millicent took aim but just as she was about to shoot, the dispenser gave way, whistled over Paddington's head and hit her control switch. She zipped chaotically back up the wire and thumped into the skylight. The jolt loosened a smoke grenade from her belt which fell, landed at the foot of the stairs and began to belch clouds of smoke. Millicent hastily put on her gas mask. Recovering his balance, Paddington turned and stared in horror at what looked like a monstrous elephant dangling on a wire and waving a gun. He screamed and ran into the kitchen, jamming the chair against the door and looking frantically for somewhere to hide. He saw the oven door was open and dived in, not realising as he did so that he'd knocked the gas on with his shoulder.

Listening through the walls, Mr Curry had heard the scream from next door. He shot up the ladder on to the roof and began scrambling across to the Browns' to rescue his beloved.

"Honey Pot? I'm coming!" he bellowed.

With one swift move, Millicent had broken the door down and burst into the kitchen, but to her anger, there was no sign of the bear. She began opening cupboards and the tumble dryer, but then suddenly caught sight of Paddington's blue duffel coat sticking out of the oven door. Creeping up silently, she flung it open – but he wasn't there either! Mr Curry stuck his head down through the skylight in the hallway.

"Fierce Eagle's here. Need a hand?"

A single petal fell from his carnation into the

stairwell where it landed on a mouse-trap and set it off. The spring pinged its cheese into the air with such force that it ricocheted off the kitchen lightshade and knocked Mrs Brown's best vase off a shelf. The vase fell onto the oven and hit the ignition button. There was a small spark, then an almighty **BOOM!!!** as the escaping gas exploded, blowing Millicent right off her feet.

The house was on fire! An alarm bell began shrieking and Millicent came round again to the sound of a concerned neighbour knocking on the front door.

"Hello? Is everything all right?" she called.

Hearing a fire engine approaching, Millicent grabbed the grenade, raced back up the zipwire and disappeared through the skylight.

Paddington fell from the kitchen ceiling where he had climbed when he decided that the oven wasn't safe enough. The sellotape had held him in place there like a giant chrysalis. The Browns and Mrs Bird arrived home shortly after to find him sitting in the middle of the rug in a pool of fire-extinguisher foam. Henry stared in dismay at the sooty wallpaper and the melted television.

"Don't worry about *me*, Mr Brown. Have a nice

day, Mr Brown!" he mimicked. "I told you we shouldn't have left him, Mary!"

"It wasn't my fault, Mr Brown," said Paddington pleadingly. "There was an elephant!"

Even Jonathan was struggling to believe him.

"It's true," said Paddington. "It had an elephant's head and a snake's body."

Mrs Bird put a hand on her forehead.

"Have you been drinking seawater?" she said.

Mary knelt down beside him.

"Paddington, tell us what really happened. We won't be cross."

"Speak for yourself," muttered Henry.

Paddington looked at them in dismay.

"I promise, I would *never* lie to you," he said, earnestly.

Even if they didn't say it to his face, it was obvious that nobody believed him and as Paddington lay in bed that night, he heard Mr and Mrs Brown arguing.

"That was the final straw, Mary. Think of the children."

"It was an accident, Henry," she said. "Paddington's the best thing that's happened to them! They don't argue, Judy's finally talking to us. They're *happy*!"

"The fact is, that bear is putting them in danger," said Henry. "And he didn't tell us the truth. How can he possibly stay here if we can't trust him?"

Paddington sat on the edge of the bed and waited anxiously for Mrs Brown's reply.

"I don't know, Henry. Perhaps when I first asked Paddington to stay, I hadn't really thought it through…"

Paddington had heard enough. He grabbed the list he'd made of all the M. Clydes, hung Aunt Lucy's luggage label back round his neck and, with one last look around the room, he put his hat on and crept out of the front door with his suitcase.

With no particular place to go, Paddington wandered out into the rainy London night. Having plodded past the trees in St James's Park, he found himself outside Buckingham Palace, where a kindly sentry guard offered him a cake and hot drink from under his bearskin hat.

"I'm sure Her Majesty would put you up for the night," said the guard. But Paddington wasn't a royal bear and although Buckingham Palace was a lot bigger than the Browns' house, he couldn't call it home, so, tipping his hat to the guard, he moved on.

Paddington made his way along the riverbank opposite St Paul's Cathedral. By now he was exhausted and, seeing a bench, he curled up and went to sleep in his duffel coat, shivering under the stars.

Chapter Eight

WRONG NUMBER

THE NEXT MORNING, Mrs Brown went upstairs to wake Paddington only to find that his room was empty. His duffel coat and hat were nowhere to be seen, his suitcase was missing and his photo of Aunt Lucy and Uncle Pastuzo was gone. There was a note on his pillow.

"Oh, Paddington," she sighed. "How am I going to tell the children?"

She went down to the kitchen to break the news.

"Why did he go?" said Jonathan. "What does the note say?"

Mary read it out.

"Dear Browns, thank you so much for having me to stay. You are a lovely family. I am very sorry about Mr Brown's toothbrush and the flood and the fire and the incident at the Geographers' Guild. I hope that now I have gone, things will be better for you all. Yours, Paddington."

Judy shook her head in disbelief.

"Better? It was so much worse without him. We're going to find him, right?"

Mary opened her mouth to reply but Henry jumped in first.

"It's better this way," he said. "He didn't really belong here."

The children looked at him in disgust.

"How can you say that?" cried Jonathan, running out of the room.

"I'm going to my room!" said Judy, storming after him.

Henry choked on his cornflakes as his wife followed the children out of the kitchen without a backwards glance.

"Mary, where are you going?"

"I just need to know that he's ok," she said, heading out of the front door.

Mrs Bird folded her arms and harrumphed.

"Looks like my intuition let me down for once," she said.

"What?" said Henry dully.

She picked up the unopened jar of marmalade on the breakfast table and waved it at him.

"You just don't get it, do you? This family needed that wee bear every bit as much as he needed us. But what do I know? I'm just a silly old woman."

"You're not that old," said Henry, realising that he was the silly one.

Mrs Bird cleared away the breakfast things.

"I'll put this marmalade back in the cupboard," she said. "In case of emergencies."

"Quite," said Henry.

That dawn, Paddington woke on the park bench surrounded by noisy pigeons. Shooing them away, he took the list of M. Clydes out of his suitcase and counted the names; there were 50. It was going to take some time to visit them all, so after a quick bite of sandwich, he set off along the Thames.

Reaching the nearest address in just under an hour, he rang the doorbell. A man opened the window, still in his pyjamas.

"Excuse me, I'm looking for Montgomery Clyde," called Paddington.

"Oh, sorry, mate. I'm Morgan Clyde," said the man.

Paddington crossed him off the list and studied his A–Z of London. Meanwhile, Mrs Brown was giving his description to the desk sergeant at the local police station.

"He's about three foot six," she said. "He's got a bright red hat on and a blue duffel coat. And he's a bear."

The sergeant shrugged.

"It's not much to go on."

"Really?"

"We'll do what we can to find him – but it's a big city."

Nobody knew that better than Paddington. He had trudged several miles already searching for the explorer and his legs were aching, but he wasn't about to give up. According to Big Ben, Mr Gruber would be having his elevenses right now. Walking was hungry work and Paddington would have done anything for a sticky bun.

By the evening, he'd only crossed a third of the names off his list, so when he reached the next address and pressed the buzzer, he really hoped it would be the one.

"Montgomery Clyde?" he said, as the door opened. It was on a short chain and there was a little old lady behind it.

"I'm Marjorie Clyde, dearie," she said. "Are you from Social Services?"

"No, Darkest Peru," said Paddington, turning away. "Sorry to have troubled you."

Paddington crossed her address off his list. He was so tired. He sat down in a bus shelter and, as he nodded off, he thought about the Browns and wondered if they missed him at all.

If he only could have seen them, he'd have had his answer.

Jonathan was alone in his room, playing half-heartedly with his fairground model. Mrs Brown was doodling bears all over her sketchbook; Judy wasn't talking to her and no one could even look at Henry. When he came home from work, he found Mary sitting on the stairs.

"There's still no news. In case you're interested," she said dejectedly.

"Right," said Henry.

Mary went upstairs to change the sheets on the little bed in the attic but she couldn't bear to wash the inky paw prints off.

Two days later, Paddington was also about to give up. He was tired and hungry, and by now he'd visited every address on his list except one. This HAD to be him – it had to be the explorer! Paddington set off in the drizzle down a dimly-lit street, looking for flat number 36. It took him a while to find it as it was above a TV shop and, shivering with cold, he pressed the buzzer.

"'Oo is it?" said a gruff voice.

Paddington called through the letterbox.

"Hello. I'm looking for Montgomery Clyde?"

"Never 'eard of him."

Paddington's whiskers crumpled.

"Oh, but you must have done. Please, I've…"

"Clear orf!" yelled the man.

Paddington went back down the stairs. He crossed off the last M. Clyde on his list, scrunched up the paper and, as the wind snatched it away, he stood by the kerb in despair. Cold and hungry, he was even wondering whether there was a spare bed at the Not An Orphanage, when a passing car splashed him. Blinking water from his eyes, he noticed that there was *another* number 36 above the dry cleaners opposite.

He ran back up the stairs to have another look at the brass numbers on the flat above the TV shop: the 6 of 36 had come loose and turned upside down. He'd been buzzing number 39 by mistake! He flew back down the stairs and ran to the real number 36. With his heart thumping, he pressed the bell.

"Hello?" answered a woman's voice.

Paddington stood on tiptoes and spoke into the entry phone.

"Hello. I'm looking for Montgomery Clyde."

"That's my father," said the voice.

Paddington's mouth fell open.

"The explorer, Montgomery Clyde?"

"That's right. You must be awfully cold. Come in."

The red light on the CCTV camera winked and

as the door opened with a buzz, he entered and waited at the bottom of the stone staircase. The woman appeared on the stairs. She seemed pleased to see him. Paddington raised his hat.

"I'm sorry to bother you, is Captain Clyde at home?"

Millicent ran her fingers through her blonde hair.

"I'm afraid not. You see, my father is dead."

All the joy drained out of Paddington's face.

"Oh! Oh, dear."

"Why do you want him?" asked Millicent.

"He once told my aunt that if we ever came to London, we'd be welcome," said Paddington. "And I suppose I was hoping that he might give me a home."

Millicent tried not to cackle. The marmalade bear she had been hunting had walked straight into her clutches.

"Oh, but *I* can do that," she said in a syrupy voice.

Paddington's eyes lit up.

"You can?"

She ran her hands through his fur. It felt kind and comforting. Perhaps it wouldn't have felt quite that way if Paddington had realised she was feeling to see how much stuffing he'd need.

"Of course," said Millicent. "A lovely specimen like you shouldn't be out on the streets. You belong somewhere very special. And I know just the place. Come along, we're going for a lovely ride."

Relieved that he'd finally found a friendly face, Paddington followed her into a waiting van. It had 'Taxi' written on one half of the sliding door, so he felt perfectly safe but as she shut it, the second half of the word slid into place so it read 'Taxidermist'. Millicent was about to drive off when Mr Curry came hurrying towards the van waving a fistful of dead flowers that looked as if they'd been taken from a road accident shrine.

"Miss Clyde! Honey Pot!" he called.

Millicent kept the engine running and wound the window down.

"What do you want?"

He thrust the bouquet at her.

"I found these tied to a lamp post and thought waste not, want not."

Millicent turned her nose up and revved the engine.

"Charming. Now if you'll excuse me."

"Where are you off to?" said Mr Curry. "Only, I notice you've got the bear in there."

"Hello, Mr Curry!" called Paddington from the back.

"And?" said Millicent, coldly.

Mr Curry pointed uncomfortably to the sign on the van.

"It's just, I er… I thought you were sending him back to Peru."

"I said I was sending him where he belongs," said Millicent. "Which in his case is the Natural History Museum."

Mr Curry looked aghast.

"But Honey Pot, that's barbaric!"

"I am not your Honey Pot, Mr Curry. And I never was," snarled Millicent. "Now take your rotten flowers and go!"

He backed away, terrified.

"*Now!*" screamed Millicent, almost reversing into him.

As Mr Curry turned and fled, Millicent screeched off with Paddington in the back seat. Moments later, the telephone rang at 32 Windsor Gardens.

"Hello?" said Henry.

"Good evening. This is an anonymous phone call," said a peculiar voice.

Henry recognised it straight away.

"Hello, Mr Curry."

"It's not Mr Curry, it's Mr… Burry. I have some news concerning the bear."

Henry listened carefully, his eyebrows knitted in a deep frown.

"Good God!" he exclaimed.

"Who is it, Henry?" called Mrs Brown.

He put his hand over the earpiece.

"It's Mr Curry pretending to be anonymous."

"It's *BURRY!*" insisted the voice on the other end.

Mary took one look at her husband's face and knew something awful had happened.

"What is it, Henry?"

"Paddington's been kidnapped!" he said.

Jonathan and Judy overheard and came rushing into the kitchen.

"Is it true?" said Jonathan.

"*Obviously!*" wailed Judy as Mr Brown fished his car keys out of the fruit bowl and headed for the front door, closely followed by Mrs Brown. Judy rushed after them while Jonathan fetched his backpack.

"Where do you think you're going?" said Mr Brown as the children got into the back of the car.

"To save Paddington!" said Judy.

"No, *we're* going to save Paddington," insisted Henry.

The children refused to get out.

"You can trust us, Dad," said Jonathan.

Mrs Bird came running down the path.

"Anchors away!" she said, clambering in with the children. "That wee bear's going to need all the help he can get."

"Put your foot down, Henry!" said Mary.

Her handbag shot off the seat as the car squealed off.

Chapter Nine

GET STUFFED

MILLICENT USHERED PADDINGTON into the Great Hall of the Natural History Museum and locked the massive doors behind them. He took a sharp intake of breath as the moonlight illuminated a dinosaur skeleton bigger than a London bus. Apart from the exhibits, the place was deserted.

"Welcome to your new home, Bear," said Millicent. "This is the Cathedral of Knowledge. Every major explorer has added to its glory. Captain

Cook brought the kangaroo from Australia, Scott brought the Emperor Penguin from Antarctica…"

"Is that Father Christmas?" asked Paddington as she hurried him past a statue of a man with a beard sitting on the landing.

"*That* is Charles Darwin," she said. "He is now immortalised through his finds. But do you see a single creature collected by my father?"

There were so many on display Paddington wasn't quite sure where to look.

"No!" said Millicent, in a voice that was seething with rage. "And I'll tell you why, Bear. Because when he saw your oh-so-precious species, he refused to collect a specimen."

"A specimen?" said Paddington, not entirely sure what that meant.

"He returned from Peru and showed his film footage to the gentlemen of the Geographers' Guild, who of course wanted a specimen to display in the museum!" Millicent snarled, and slapped her own forehead. "But oh, no — my father said you bears were *intelligent* and *civilised*, and he would never harm you! The Guild revoked his membership on the spot. Daddy could have been rich and famous! But he threw it all away and got a job in a petting zoo." She almost spat her last words.

"Sounds nice," said Paddington, looking at the prehistoric monkey skulls.

Millicent narrowed her eyes.

"Well, it wasn't! We lived above the donkeys. I had to walk through their stinking pen on my way to school and all the children used to mock me."

She chanted in a sing-song voice like a six year old, "Dung breath! Dung breath! Millicent's got dung breath!"

She pounded up the next flight of stairs.

"That's when I realised my father had been wrong to do what he did," she said. "And I vowed that one day I would get hold of the specimen that ruined my childhood and put it here where it belongs!"

She whipped a dust sheet off an enormous specimen cabinet adorned with a plaque; it was engraved with the words *Ursus Marmalada*. The fur on the back of Paddington's neck stood on end.

"That's right, Bear," said Millicent, grabbing him by the scruff of his neck. "I'm going to stuff you!"

Paddington managed to wriggle out of her grasp. He ran off, but she pulled out her dart gun, aimed and fired. This time, she hit the target. Paddington gave a yelp, clutched his bottom and with a big yawn, he tumbled down the stairs.

Moments later, the Browns pulled up outside the museum, a little carsick but impressed by Henry's motor racing skills. They jumped out of the car – there was a light burning in the upper window. Mrs Bird rooted around in her handbag and pulled out a telescope. She could see someone – a woman – carrying Paddington over to a table. He didn't appear to be moving.

"Bear in the crow's nest," she said.

"What's he doing? Is he okay?" said Mrs Brown anxiously.

Mrs Bird had another squint and thought she could detect signs of life.

"He's sleeping but not in a good way," she said, collapsing the telescope. "All hands on deck. There's not a moment to lose."

"How are we going to get in?" said Jonathan.

Henry cast his eye over the imposing building adorned with terracotta birds and beasts of all description. It was home to some of the rarest specimens in the world.

"It'll be locked like a fortress," he said. "With alarms and cameras and…"

"Sewers!" said Judy suddenly.

Everyone looked at her blankly.

"Didn't you say they could take you anywhere in the city, Mum?"

"I did, didn't I? And they do! Good thinking, Judy!" said Mrs Brown, searching on the pavement for a manhole. Judy turned to Jonathan who was checking the contents of his backpack.

"Mum just called me by my name."

"Weird," he said. "Where's Mrs Bird going?"

She was heading for the Security Gatehouse. Mrs Bird had a trick up her sleeve, not to mention a bottle of sailor-strength rum. Inside was a security guard with a Rottweiler dozing at his feet. She tapped on the window and put on a feeble voice.

"Excuse me, young man?"

Seeing an elderly lady standing outside shivering in her shawl, he opened the door.

"You all right, pet?"

"Could you help a frail old woman?" said Mrs

Bird pitifully. "I've missed the bus. It's so cold, there's icebergs floating in ma blood."

The guard helped her up the steps.

"Come and sit by the fire for a bit."

"Oh, my bunions," she complained. "I'm seventy five, you know."

Mrs Bird had quickly whispered her plan to Henry. He hastily explained it to the rest of the family and the Browns crouched down by a wall, a security camera standing between them and their destination.

"Wait 'til it moves," said Henry.

"I do hope Mrs Bird's all right in there," said Mary.

"She sailed round Cape Horn single-handed, Mum!" said Judy.

Mrs Bird slipped off her shoes. Warming her feet by the fire, she studied the bank of monitors and worked out which lever operated the CCTV camera overlooking the manhole. Then she produced her bottle of rum and waved it at the guard.

"Do you fancy a wee nip of anti-freeze for the old pacemaker, laddie?"

"Not while I'm on duty," he smiled.

Mrs Bird unscrewed the cap and took a swig.

"Too strong for you, eh?"

"Fighting talk," he grinned, relenting. "I'll get us a couple of glasses."

As he turned his back, Mrs Bird reached over and shifted the joystick on the CCTV.

"The camera's moving away, Dad," said Jonathan.

"Let's go!" said Henry.

They all ran to the manhole cover, lifted it between them and helped each other down the ladder into the old sewer below.

"Why on earth would anyone want to kidnap Paddington?" puffed Mrs Brown, running to keep up with Henry. "If that woman hurts him, I'll never forgive her."

"Hurt him? Over my dead body," said Henry.

But even as he spoke, Millicent was pulling out her knife and walking over to Paddington, who was snoring on the table in the secret stuffing room. She sharpened the blade lovingly, crooning a little song: "How much is that Bear-y in the window? The one with the staring glass eyes..."

"Nearly there!" said Mrs Brown, running along the sewer tunnel. It was dark and dank but apart from a bit of sludge, there was no raw sewage.

"This place is amazing," said Judy. "I thought it would stink… what's up, Dad?"

Henry had reached the manhole cover directly under the museum and was trying to force it open with his shoulder.

"It won't shift," he said. "It must be locked. Blast it."

Jonathan reached into his backpack and pulled out an old box full of test tubes, vials of liquid and coloured powder.

"That's my old chemistry set!" said Henry.

"It's lethal, is what it is," said Jonathan, rigging up a charge. "You did say blast it. Got a light, Judy?"

She felt in her pockets and gave him a box of matches.

"Darling?" said Mrs Brown in distress. "I never knew you smoked?"

"They're for lighting joss sticks," said Judy hurriedly. "When I meditate."

"You do? Oh, that's good for stress," said Mrs Brown, nodding in approval.

Jonathan lit the fuse and counted down.

"5-4-3-2…"

Henry waved his arms frantically.

"Jonathan!"

"What, Dad?"

"Go for it, son!"

They ran to the bottom of the stairs, put their hands over their ears and waited for the boom... **BANG!!!** The manhole shattered like a poppadom.

"That did the trick!" said Jonathan, poking his head through the blackened hole in the floor of the Great Hall. "Hey, I can see the diplodocus from here!"

They climbed out and ran over to a fuse box hidden behind an extinct Giant Moa from New Zealand.

"Kill the lights," said Henry.

Jonathan reached for the switch.

Millicent raised her knife above Paddington's sleeping body. She was about to strike when the room was suddenly plunged into darkness. She slammed the knife into the counter beside him and fumbled in a drawer for her torch. Then, yanking the stuffed rhino's tail that opened the door from the inside, she marched out, flashing the beam.

The Browns hid at the bottom of the grand staircase. They held their breath until she passed, then, creeping out of the shadows, they hurried up the stairs to the top floor where Mrs Bird had last seen Paddington through her telescope.

"It's at the end of that corridor," said Henry, pressing his nose to a glass door barring their way. He rattled the handle; it was locked.

"You'll have to blow it, Jonathan," he said. "Mind out, Mary."

Jonathan shook an empty tin at him.

"I can't. I've used all the explosive."

Thinking on his feet, Henry opened the window and leaned out.

"Henry, you are NOT going out there!" said Mrs Brown.

"Do it, Dad!" said Jonathan.

Henry took off his overcoat and handed it to his wife.

"Someone's got to," he said. "And that someone is me."

He took Mrs Brown in his arms and kissed her.

"My hero!" she gasped.

"Ugh!" grinned Judy, but as Henry stepped out onto the ledge, she stopped.

"Seriously, Dad. Get back in. It's snowing."

"Sensible and boring?" he said jauntily, clinging to a stone carving of a snake around the window as he side-stepped along. Against his better judgement, he looked down. The cars below looked no bigger than Dinky Toys.

"Actually, this is insane," he muttered, inching back towards the open window.

He bent his knees to climb back in but seeing his family watching him with such adoration, he straightened up again.

"Dad is properly cool," said Jonathan.

"He certainly is," gushed Mrs Brown.

Henry sighed. He was going to have to do this. He edged his way back towards the balcony, blinking the snowflakes from his eyes. He was almost there! Reaching out to grasp a stone-carved octopus tentacle, he realised his mistake too late – it was an icicle. It snapped off in his hand.

"OMG!" shrieked Judy. "Dad's fallen!"

"Henry?" cried Mrs Brown, craning out of the window.

He was clinging to a gargoyle a few feet below.

"I'm all right, Mary," he said, pulling himself back up.

"Mum, is Dad somehow related to Spiderman?" said Jonathan.

"I'm beginning to wonder..." she said.

Henry reached the window of the stuffing room and looked in. Through the gloom, he could see Paddington lying still on the table, surrounded by sharp instruments. Was he too late? He tapped urgently on the pane.

"Paddington...! Paddington!"

Nothing. No movement.

"Paddington?"

No response. Mr Brown felt his eyes prickle. This was all his fault. He wouldn't blame his family if they hated him but right now, nobody hated him more than himself.

"I'm so sorry," he sniffed.

Paddington shifted on the table and raised his head.

"Is that you, God?" he called blearily. "You sound much more like Mr Brown than I'd imagined."

"It *is* Mr Brown," hissed Henry. "Look behind you!"

Paddington sat up. He was half-awake, but when he saw who was on the balcony, he thought he was still dreaming. He rubbed his eyes.

"Mr Brown! What are you doing there?"

"We've come to rescue you," he said. "Mr Curry explained everything. I'm so sorry I didn't believe you. I wish you'd never left. I want you to live with us."

Paddington brushed away a tear.

"Do you really?"

"We *all* do," smiled Henry.

Meanwhile, Millicent had discovered the gaping hole in the hall where the manhole cover had exploded by almost falling down it. Spotting the mucky footprints leading up to the fuse box, she found to her fury that someone had turned the power off... which must have happened after she'd locked the door... which meant there was somebody still in the building!

"Sabotage," she hissed, hitting the alarm.

She flicked the power switch. As the lights came back on, automatic security shutters began to lower on the doors and windows, including the ones in the stuffing room.

"Quick, Paddington!" yelled Henry through the window. "Get out of there!"

Chapter Ten

HOME

PADDINGTON ROLLED OFF the table and hurried towards the lowering shutter as fast as he could, shaking his head to clear the grogginess. As he dived beneath it, his hat fell off. He went to grab it, but was too slow and the shutter closed on his paw. He was trapped! The pain took his breath away but the thought of ending up in the specimen cabinet gave him the burst of strength he needed. Struggling frantically, he pulled himself free.

Paddington examined his paw. Apart from one claw, nothing was broken and, trying to ignore the throbbing, he raced along the Upper Gallery of the Great Hall.

"You!" yelled Millicent from below.

She raised her tranquilliser gun, but as she fired, Paddington leapt over the balustrade, landed on the back of the diplodocus and ran down its spine, as darts ricocheted off its skeleton.

Tumbling off the end of its tail, he ran under a stone arch and through a door marked *Specimens*. With Millicent hot on his heels, he zigzagged past countless jars filled with pickled animals – everything from slugs to ceolacanths – their dead eyes staring at him, faces distorted against the glass.

Wondering whether he was in fact in the middle of a nightmare, Paddington pinched himself. To his disappointment, he was wide awake. He sped up, burst out of the door at the far end, skidded down the corridor and ran into the nearest room.

It was a dead end – a small, windowless space filled with a boiler and bits of cleaning equipment. Paddington turned to go back the way he came, but it was too late; he could hear Millicent's heels clacking towards him round the corner. He slammed the door shut and locked it.

"Give up, Bear. There's no escape," she said from outside.

He looked round desperately for a way out – the only route seemed to be the steel-lined chimney above the boiler, but he would never be able to climb it; it was too slippery even for his claws.

Suddenly, he noticed a pair of objects propped up in a recharging unit on the wall. He recognised them straight away: cordless Dust Busters! These ones were much bigger than Mrs Bird's. Paddington turned one on to test the suction, and almost disappeared up the nozzle. Hearing the sound of the vacuum, Millicent peered through the keyhole.

"What are you doing?" she sneered. "Trying to make a clean get away?"

Feeling to make sure the boiler was cold, Paddington fetched the other Dust Buster and turned them both on. Holding one in each paw, he stood under the open chimney vent and looked up. High above, he could see the moon shining like a ten pence piece. It was a long way off, but he had to aim for it, or he was stuffed.

Paddington steeled himself. Using the suction

from the Dust Busters, he clamped himself to the inside of the vent. By switching them on and off alternately, he began to climb slowly up the chimney, paw over paw. After a few yards, he'd got the knack of it and was feeling much more positive when he heard the time switch click below. The boiler had come on.

Flames began to rise from beneath as Paddington increased his pace. He remembered the warm welcome the explorer had promised – it was a lot hotter than he would have liked right now, but the thought of going home with the Browns kept him reaching for the stars.

Mr Brown had climbed in through an open window and was running down the corridor searching for Paddington when he bumped into Mary and the children coming the other way.

"Henry, there you are. I was so worried!" said Mrs Brown.

"Where's Paddington?" asked Jonathan.

Henry cast his eyes around wildly.

"I don't know!"

They looked at each other helplessly, then Judy heard something.

"Shh! Clang… clang… clang," she intoned, cupping her ear.

"Is that Mandarin, darling?" said Mrs Brown.

Judy pointed up above.

"Can't you hear it?"

They all listened; there it was… a metal clang… followed by another.

"He's heading for the roof," said Judy.

She ran towards the lift.

"No, this way," insisted Henry, leading them to the fire escape.

"Statistically safer, Dad?" asked Jonathan, running after him.

"Quicker."

As the Browns clattered up the spiral staircase, Paddington had almost reached the top of the chimney. He only had a few feet to go when the Dust Buster in his left paw spluttered and died. Dangling by one arm, he dropped it; three full seconds later, it fell into the boiler below and melted.

Paddington gulped. One false move and he was toast. Realising that the Dust Buster in his right paw was about to lose suction too, he flipped himself up and landed on top of it. It began to slide down under his weight; setting his jaw and focussing on the top of the chimney, he took a leap.

He fell short. Scrabbling to get a grip on the smooth sides, his claws screeched against the steel as he began to fall. He closed his eyes and as he prayed for Uncle Pastuzo to carry him to Bear Heaven, someone put their arms around him.

"Up you come," said Jonathan, leaning over the chimney as Mr Brown held him firmly round the waist.

"We've got you!" said Judy, gripping her father while Mrs Brown held onto her.

They pulled Paddington out onto the roof.

"Are you okay?" asked Jonathan.

Paddington sat in the snow, gazing at the pigeons on the chimney pots.

"They are *not* having my marmalade sandwich," he said dazedly.

"He's okay," smiled Judy.

Henry helped Paddington onto his feet.

"Come on. Let's find Mrs Bird and get out of here."

"Not. So. Fast," said Millicent.

Paddington spun round. There she was at the other end of the roof, pointing her gun at him.

"No!" cried Jonathan and Judy.

"Hand over the bear," said Millicent, stepping closer.

Mrs Brown stood in front of Paddington and folded her arms.

"No. We can't do that. He's family."

Millicent laughed in her face.

"Family? You're not even the same species!"

Paddington hung his head. Being a bear, he worried that the Browns would never truly accept him as one of their own. But then Henry stepped forward.

"True, we're not the same," he said, "and when I first met Paddington, I wanted nothing to do with him…"

He faltered for a second. Out of the corner of his eye he could see Mary looking at him just like she used to before the children were born.

"But my wonderful wife opened her heart to him and so did my incredible children…"

"Respect," said Jonathan, bumping fists with Judy.

"…and at last, I have too," said Henry. "It doesn't matter where Paddington came from or that he's a bear with a peculiar marmalade habit. We love him. That makes him family and families stick together."

"You go, Dad!" said Judy.

Henry raised his fist like a general and with great gusto, he drew his speech to an end.

"If you want Paddington, you'll have to take us all!"

"Okay then," shrugged Millicent, cocking her gun at his head.

Henry tried hard to keep a stiff upper lip.

"Ah. When I say all…"

"I've never stuffed a human," said Millicent brightly. "But how hard can it be?"

Just then Paddington came out from behind the Browns and walked towards her. Jonathan tried to pull him back, but he kept going.

"There's a good little bear," grinned Millicent.

"No!" wailed Judy.

There was a loud coo as the pigeon from Paddington station landed on a nearby rooftop. It seemed to be able to smell marmalade from miles away and would stop at nothing to get it. Suddenly, Paddington had an idea.

"May I have one last request?" he asked.

"What is it?" snapped Millicent.

"I'd like a sandwich, please. There's one in my hat."

He took it out and held it up by the crust.

"Go on then." She rolled her eyes.

Seeing its prize, the pigeon rose up, flapping. Timing it perfectly, Paddington hurled the sandwich at Millicent, and a whole flock of pigeons descended and swarmed across the roof after the crumbs.

Engulfed by hungry birds, Millicent stumbled backwards towards the edge of the roof. For a second, she teetered on the edge in her heels and was almost about to fall when a sudden gust of wind blew her back. Whirling her arms like windmills, she caught her balance.

"Nice try, Bear," she sneered, raising her gun.

Paddington squeezed his eyes shut and awaited his fate. There was a loud bang and a scream. He opened his eyes again quickly. A skylight had swung open and knocked Millicent clean off the roof.

Mrs Bird's head poked out of the hatch. "I had a feeling in ma water I'd find you here," she hiccupped.

The Browns gawped at her, speechless.

"Why are you all looking at me?" she said as Mrs Brown helped pull her out.

"Get me down!" yelled a voice from below.

Mrs Bird looked confused. She weaved across the

roof and looked over the edge; there was Millicent, dangling from a flagpole.

"Well, tickle my tartan," exclaimed Mrs Bird, knee-bobbing back to the Browns.

Paddington flew into her arms.

"Mrs Bird, you saved me!" he said, as the rest of the Browns joined him.

"Easy," she said. "Away with you. I've got a splitting headache."

But while she pretended not to like a fuss, Mrs Bird took her time to let them go.

Far away from Darkest Peru, Paddington Brown was sharing his marmalade-making skills with his new family. He'd given everyone a particular job to do and they were all enjoying themselves no end.

Mrs Brown was peeling oranges. Jonathan and Judy were in charge of pips and pith. Mr Brown was chopping and while Mrs Bird sterilised the jam jars, Paddington stood on a stool and stirred the pot with a big wooden spoon.

"How's it looking, Paddington?" said Mary.

"It smells pretty good," said Judy.

Paddington waved his spoon in the air, flicking a sticky chunk onto his hat.

"Just one sandwich contains all the vitamins and minerals a bear needs," he reminded them as Mrs Bird did her best to clean the brim.

"So I can cut out eating vegetables?" said Jonathan.

Mrs Bird flicked him playfully with her tea towel.

"He said bear, not boy!"

Paddington clambered down off the stool.

"There's something missing. Excuse me a moment."

He disappeared into the hall, returned with an item of footwear and dangled it over the pot by one lace.

"That's my shoe," said Mr Brown.

"It's the secret ingredient, Mr Brown," said Paddington earnestly.

Henry thought about it for a second. He'd only bought those shoes because they were sensible. Now he looked at them properly, they were rather boring.

"Oh, go on then!" he said.

Paddington dropped the shoe into the mixture with a satisfying plop. As it came to a rolling boil, an intoxicating aroma filled the room; a delicious blend of fruit, forest and family. The Browns inhaled deeply and swooned.

"*Wo…w*!" said Jonathan.

"Every family should have a marmalade day," said Mary.

"And a bear," said Judy.

"Oh, especially a bear," said Henry fondly. "Paddington, where are you?"

He was under the table eating a marmalade sandwich.

"I'm *home, Mr Brown," said Paddington.

A letter arrived for Aunt Lucy at the Home for Retired Bears in Lima. Seeing the London postcode, she opened it with shaking paws, though by the time she'd read to the end, she felt happier than she had in a very long time.

Dear Aunt Lucy,

Sorry I haven't written for a while but a lot has been happening. I was almost stuffed, but don't worry, everything is fine. Captain Clyde's daughter wanted me for a specimen but Mrs Bird threw her off the roof. She can't harm me now because the judge gave her the worst punishment she could imagine — sweeping up donkey dung in a petting zoo!

The good news is I'm back living with the

Browns. Mrs Bird says everything is set to fair and it has had a remarkable effect on her knees. Judy's embarrassment has cleared up and she has let Mrs Brown meet Tony. Mr Brown is making a rocket with Jonathan which is great except Jonathan is worried his dad will blow the bedroom up using too much nitro-glycerine. I have just heard a loud explosion but Mr Brown is laughing and saying Houston may have a problem, whoever he is.

I'm so glad you sent me here, Aunt Lucy. Mrs Brown says that in London, everyone is different – but that means everyone can fit in. I think she must be right because I really do feel at home here now. I may not look like anyone else but that is Okay. Because I am a bear. A bear called Paddington.

I am just off to play snowballs with Jonathan and Judy, and afterwards Mr Brown has promised me a ride on the back of his Kawasaki 850, but I promise to write soon.

Lots of love, Paddington Brown x